LAZY WATER

A Novel

GWEN ENQUIST

Order this book online at www.trafford.com/07-2502
or email orders@trafford.com

Most Trafford titles are also available at major online book retailers.

Cover design/artwork by:
Robert Dufour Works Consulting
Powell River, B.C.
robert@worksconsulting.ca

© Copyright 2008 Gwen Enquist.

All rights reserved. No part of this publication may be reproduced, stored in a retrieval system, or transmitted, in any form or by any means, electronic, mechanical, photocopying, recording, or otherwise, without the written prior permission of the author.

Note for Librarians: A cataloguing record for this book is available from Library and Archives Canada at www.collectionscanada.ca/amicus/index-e.html

Printed in Victoria, BC, Canada.

ISBN: 978-1-4251-5585-8

We at Trafford believe that it is the responsibility of us all, as both individuals and corporations, to make choices that are environmentally and socially sound. You, in turn, are supporting this responsible conduct each time you purchase a Trafford book, or make use of our publishing services. To find out how you are helping, please visit www.trafford.com/responsiblepublishing.html

Our mission is to efficiently provide the world's finest, most comprehensive book publishing service, enabling every author to experience success. To find out how to publish your book, your way, and have it available worldwide, visit us online at www.trafford.com/10510

Trafford
PUBLISHING

www.trafford.com

North America & international
toll-free: 1 888 232 4444 (USA & Canada)
phone: 250 383 6864 ♦ fax: 250 383 6804
email: info@trafford.com

The United Kingdom & Europe
phone: +44 (0)1865 722 113 ♦ local rate: 0845 230 9601
facsimile: +44 (0)1865 722 868 ♦ email: info.uk@trafford.com

10 9 8 7 6 5 4 3 2

To my brother, David, for his insightful suggestions and to my husband, Ray, and son, Douglas, for their support in the most important ways.

· Chapter 1 ·

The last thing Joe expected to see when he came out of the pizza shop was a man pulling a gun on a woman in the parking lot. By any standard, buying a pizza is a non-event, innocuous, like buying paint, which was his next stop. And it wasn't that Joe was a stranger to violent events, living in Toronto as he did, but the fact that this parking lot was in the small city of his childhood made him question what he had seen.

Joe lowered his sunglasses for a clearer view and, for one startled, adrenaline-spiked moment, was sure he saw a gun raised to target a young woman. When the shooter stepped back, Joe could see that the man was aiming at the woman's face with a finger pointing forward, the parody of a gun directed at her head. He squeezed the trigger action and mouthed a soft bang. There was such contempt in the action and intent to intimidate the young woman — whose small, pale face suggested vulnerability — that Joe couldn't stand still and watch as the woman panicked. He moved away from the store and towards her, ready to help.

The woman swung around — clearly as confused as Joe had been about the finger-gun — and crashed into a shopping cart, which clattered into a half-circle spin. The man's raised hand continued in an upward arc and he slicked his dark hair. He moved across the parking lot with the easy glide of a predator and stepped into a silver Lexus convertible. He saluted the woman in a mockery of goodwill. The engine roared to life and the tires grabbed asphalt as the car screeched into traffic.

The woman's knees buckled and she sank to the ground, grit and gravel searing her bare legs. She wrapped her arms around her head and pulled into her body, as if to shield herself.

Her breaths came in rapid gasps, cleansing her body of its terror. Just as her trembling eased, Joe's hand touched her shoulder. With fear still too close to the surface, she shrieked and pulled away.

"I'm sorry. I'm sorry." Joe withdrew his hand and stepped back. "I thought you might be hurt. I didn't mean to scare you."

"Don't…I'm…don't. I'm… all right." She struggled to stand. Joe stretched his hand to help. She waved it away, rejecting contact.

Joe's tall, broad-shouldered shape blocked the late afternoon sun. It glimmered around him creating a silhouette that softened the impact of his looming presence.

"Is there anything I can do?" he said. He watched the woman, more like a girl, he thought — she was so slight — a cotton T-shirt clinging to her small breasts and outlining her slender ribcage and waist. She brushed dirt from her legs; a bead of blood swelled and leaked over her knee. Her face was sweat-streaked and she pushed limp, blond hair away from her eyes. Perspiration stains circled her under-arms.

She cleared her throat. "I'm okay. Thanks." Her voice was weak. "I'll be fine," she said. "It's superficial." She pulled at her cotton denim skirt, pressing it to its full length just above her knees. She scanned the parking lot, alert to the possibility that a threat still hovered there. Her eyes came back to the speaker. Close-cropped dark hair topped a square face while beads of light bounced off the edges of Serengeti sunglasses. A blue

T-shirt imprinted on the whitening sunlight. His strong legs still bore their bleached winter whiteness, stretched beneath khaki cargo shorts and ended in leather sandals.

"Damn those wobbly shopping carts, anyway," she said.

Shopping carts be damned, Joe thought. It was the threat and it scared *her* wobbly. "Perhaps the store could help you? I can get someone." Lines of concern creased his brow. He made a move in the direction of the store.

"No! No. I'm fine. Don't trouble yourself." She gathered her purse and took a faltering step towards a white Echo.

"Wait," he said, startling her. Joe came out of the sun's glare and looked at her more closely. "Do I know you? Aren't you Amelia? Amelia Compton?"

She turned towards him. "Do I know you?"

He removed his sunglasses. "Joe Bennett. I know it goes back a few years, but we did know each other. Vedder Elementary? Or was it Sardis Senior?"

Joe saw recognition in her face. Amelia Compton's wary smile quickly disappeared as memories clicked into place. Her mouth formed a soft oh. Her mind was tracking what she knew about him, remembering that he'd left town quickly after graduation and hadn't been back since. Now here he was in the Safeway parking lot.

She nodded, her mouth a hard line. "Not school. Our fathers." She attempted toughness, pulling her body straight and tight, but heat waves drifting off the asphalt and the 'gunman's' psychic games combined to defeat her. "I don't know why you've come back," she said. "There's only wreckage left. You're much too late." She limped the short distance to her car and slammed the door. That gesture drained the last bit of anger in her and she accelerated slowly from the parking lot.

Joe stood for a moment watching her car disappear. So, that was Amelia Compton. He'd almost forgotten about her. She used

7

to be just a skinny kid, more easily forgotten than the petite and pretty woman she was now. It was harder to forget her accountant father, Owen Compton, charged with fraud and conspiracy to defraud along with Joe's father. Joe had been gone from town for thirty years and hadn't expected a welcome parade. But neither did he expect rude dismissal from someone who hardly knew him. The sins of the father visited on the son? Clearly Amelia Compton hadn't survived untouched.

Joe admitted ignorance of the events of recent years. He'd wanted nothing to do with the old man even before his downfall. Let Nathan deal with his own sabotaged life. Best to cut away rot, move on and try to heal. Maybe Amelia Compton had a right to her anger. How many lives had Nathan Bennett wrecked along with his own? A flutter of unease stirred in his chest.

After buying the paint and collecting the pizza, he headed across the parking lot to his rental car. With one hand holding paint cans and juggling the pizza box, he managed the remote locking system, catching the pizza before it slid to the ground. When he was a kid nobody ever locked their car.

"Hey, Joe. Joey."

A tall man carrying excess poundage around his waist, shouted from across the lot. His face had reddened with exertion. By the time he caught up to Joe he was wiping sweat from his face.

"I heard you were in town. It's not even hard to recognize you, you lucky bastard. You've hardly changed since we graduated." He extended his hand. "Scott Nicols. I know you don't recognize me. Too much good living's happened." He smiled and patted his belly.

Joe could see the early features of his childhood friend in the green eyes and freckled complexion. Scott was larger and had less hair but the easy friendliness that characterized him was still there.

"Scott. My god. So good to see you." Joe pumped his hand.

"I was going to call when I had a chance. Mom told me you were still around."

"Oh, yeah. A lifer here. Doing okay. I'm running a real estate office. We're in the old McGregor building."

"Good. Good."

"Are you here for long?"

"A couple of weeks, at least. I'm helping Mom get the house ready to sell. Her name's on a list for the Lakeview Manor care facility."

"Oh, god. Time's the enemy. It doesn't seem time for our parents to need that kind of help."

"She had a stroke a few months ago. Left her with problems. She gets around but needs people in to do things," Joe said.

"Well, I hear Lakeview's a good place." Scott hesitated, shook his head slowly. "I can't believe you're here. After, what? 30 years?"

Joe nodded. "All of that," he said.

"I know your joined the air force but didn't hear much more. Are you still in the service?"

"No. I did 20 years. I was lucky, got selected for pilot training. Now I'm flying for Air Canada."

"Hey, that sounds great. Where are you based?"

"Toronto. I've been there ten years now."

Scott waited a beat. "Any family with you?"

"No. Just me," Joe replied. "My son's in Toronto with his mother."

"Listen," Scott said, "are you going to be around for a while?"

"I've got two weeks." He indicated the paint. "I hope I can get the major house repairs done in that time."

"What about your father, Joe? Are we still tight enough that I can ask? Nobody says much."

"You can ask. I really don't know much. I haven't seen him yet. Mom's not going out as much now."

"Well, listen. Let's talk about this another time. Say! Could you come out to the lake tomorrow? We're throwing some steaks on the fire and chugging some beer. Why don't you come? You'll know most everybody. Marion — I married Marion Thatcher — you remember her — anyway, come late afternoon and we'll really catch up."

"Okay. I'll be there. Still that place on Heron Bay Road?"

"Yeah, same place. Oh, this is great. Everybody'll be glad to see you."

Joe put out his hand to shake Scott's. "Thanks, Scott. See you tomorrow."

With enough building repair supplies to get his work started, Joe pulled into his mother's driveway a few minutes later. The Sycamore Street house was in an old established neighbourhood. All the houses on the street had been original to an older City of Chilliwack and the age of the trees made it a picturesque and comfortable place to live. Joe had lived here to age 17.

A wood-plank porch ran across the front of the house. Two modest columns flanked the stairs and supported the shingled roof. Rose bushes grew along the skirting of the porch, their pink and yellow blossoms lying limply against the weathered wood. Their stems were long and wispy. Joe could tell they hadn't been pruned in a couple of years.

"Mom," he shouted as he opened the door. "I'm back and I found just about everything," he added.

He walked quickly down the hallway, a passage far too dark for a bright summer day. The hallway had never been bright but the years had eroded the paint to drabness. Joe almost reached for the light switch but lost the thought when he reached the openness of the kitchen. The sun was still high in the late afternoon sky and spilled white light into the room.

Vera Bennett stood at the sink, pressed up against the counter, her left arm in a sling. Her functioning right hand was trying to wash carrots. A grey-haired woman stood at the counter, her hand resting beside on a casserole dish of steaming scalloped potatoes.

"Hello," the woman said, "you must be Joe." She extended her plump arm and thick fingers to Joe.

Joe returned the greeting. "Yes. Joe."

"I'm Marika Webber. I live next door. I brought some scalloped potatoes to help with supper." Marika Webber's open face smiled at Joe, eager in its neighbourliness. She was full-bodied woman with a deep bosomy chest designed to comfort tearful children and the broken-hearted. Her grey hair hung down her back in a single braid as round as a baby's thigh.

"Marika helps," Vera offered. "She brings good muffins too." Vera coughed on accumulated saliva, had trouble clearing it and choked until Marika intervened. Marika held tissues to Vera's face and helped her towards a chair. "Sit here, Vera."

Joe took the carrot from his mother's hand and Marika helped Vera sit at the table. With her right hand manoeuvring a quad cane, Vera pulled her left leg behind her the few steps to the chair. Marika guided her, hands cradled around Vera's hips. As she moved, her small body failed to raise an outline against the loose cotton shift. She seemed so insubstantial that Joe caught his breath.

"Thanks for helping," Joe said. With a nod at the pizza box he said, "I'll admit I'm not much of a cook. But Mom doesn't need to do it for me either."

"Mom, you don't need to do this," Joe repeated. Joe nodded towards the food preparation. He sat across from Vera at the table. Up close to her, the air around her smelled faintly organic, like fallen leaves after an autumn rain. Joe struggled with this unsettling notion.

Marika stood up. "Well, I'll head home. Pleased to meet you, Joe. If you need anything just holler. Bye, Vera. I'll be here for our crib game Friday night." She waved herself out.

Vera's eyes followed Marika out of the room. "Neighbour. Marika Webber. Next door." Joe leaned across the table, listening carefully to Vera's slurred speech. "She helps me sometimes," Vera stated.

"And plays crib too?"

"Yes." It came out as yesh, the words mildly distorted by slack muscles. Vera gestured at the food. "I wanted to make dinner — for you." She settled her paralyzed arm in her lap and sat facing her son. "Oh," she said, her voice anguished; Vera pressed her lips together to stop their quivering. Her mouth drooped slightly to the left and there was a glistening streak of saliva tracking from its corner and ending at her chin. Tears bloomed in her eyes.

"Mom, what you can't do now doesn't really count in any tally I know. What you've done in the past counts for a lot more." He leaned back into his chair. He felt his throat tighten. His words sat there in the air. After a 30-year-absence from this house, it took him only hours to condemn his father and have his mother in tears.

"Mom, I remember all those hours you spent at the church, polishing woodwork, serving teas and you were always volunteering to bake and cook for people. I even remember you taking meals to a family who were all in bed with flu. You went there three times a day for a whole week. You've done so much for others. You remember that?"

Vera gave a slow nod. "The Carpenters. Millie upset 'cause she couldn't look after her family."

"There you go. It's the same thing. Let other people help *you* when *you* need it."

Vera let two tears slide down her cheeks.

Joe passed his hand through his hair and sat at the table opposite his mother. He moved his hand towards her but didn't complete the touch that would comfort each of them. "You've done your share, Mom. Here. Look. I brought supper." He retrieved the large pizza box from the counter and opened it in front of her on the table.

Vera's face brightened. "I thought we were going to cook. And I thought you went for groceries." Vera looked questioningly at the pizza. Joe felt a nudge in his stomach, knowing he had blundered with the pizza — he should have picked Chinese take-out. Would he have to cut it up for her? Were those food stains on her clothes? How did he know what was right?

"Tonight we relax and talk about your new life. Tomorrow … maybe I'll cook." He grinned and wiggled his eyebrows. "Think you can handle it?"

"I've handled more than questionable cooking, haven't I?" she slurred.

"Yes. I know." Joe was slow to smile at his mother; she was slow to respond. And each of them held it a moment too long.

ಞ

By the time Amelia pulled into her driveway she was exhausted. Anger and fear in equal proportion had left her limp. Whenever she was defeated like this she often felt she hadn't lived up to her name. Amelia. Surely the name of a matriarch who wields control over a household. Today she felt like the diminutive Mel she'd always been — easily intimidated by her ex-husband, Dono. Not that a scenario with a gun pointed at her wasn't provocation enough to collapse into jelly. She'd reacted exactly as he's hoped she would, by shrinking into herself and losing any sense of confidence she'd acquired over the last two years without him.

She sat in the car for a few minutes, only stirring when Ty shouted from the doorway. "Mom! Mom, what are you doing? Why don't you come in?" Ty's small face leaned around the screen door; he let it slam shut as he stood on the porch. Mel looked up at her son, his thinness etched against the sun's glare. She gathered

13

her purse and inhaled evenly, pulling herself together enough to climb out of the car.

"Hi, sweetie." Mel made her face smile. The effort was like pulling Play Doh into an agreeable shape. Dono's effect dragged at her spirit and her body.

"Hey, Mom," Ty chirped. His voice was high and excited, his face open and expectant, shining with a light sheen of sweat. "Did you bring the video?"

Mel faltered, remembered her promise. "Oh, Ty," she said. Her hand went to her face and she scrubbed at the dried sweat. "I'm so sorry. I forgot." She sat on the step, motioning Ty down beside her. He planted his elbows on his knees, then his narrow face atop his closed fists. She put her arm across his shoulders and pulled him to her. She sighed. "I forgot. I think it's all the heat." With her other hand she brushed hair from his brow, trying to wipe away the disappointment. "Anyway, it's too hot for videos. Why don't we go swimming instead? Where's Grandma? We could pack a picnic and go to the beach."

Ty squirmed under her embrace. His elfin face was solemn and his brow furrowed. He weighed the merits of being cranky against swimming and of having soft ice cream at the beach food concession.

"Yeah. Swimming," he decided. He jumped up and ran into the house before Mel could move. The screen door slammed behind him. "Grandma, Gram," he shouted. "We're going to the beach."

Mel stood, the scrape on her knee twinged with pain. The wooden porch creaked with each step. It was dried out and shaky but this house was the best she could afford. She had tried to talk the landlord into doing some exterior painting but he wouldn't budge unless she could pay more rent. Mel considered buying the paint herself. She didn't think the owner would object to that. All she needed was time and energy.

Edie Compton stood in the kitchen, running water over

lettuce in the sink. A bibbed apron hung over her shoulders, the ties dangling loosely at the back. She looked damp, as if she were melting and would soon become a puddle on the worn lino floor.

Mel always felt closed in when she came into the kitchen. She was dwarfed by the large mahogany dining set with buffet and hutch that dominated the space. Its elegance showcased the dreariness of the room rather than adding fineness to its décor. Edie had refused to part with these precious pieces when her house was sold. An equally huge four-poster bed pressed against the walls of Edie's bedroom. It was what she hung onto of her early life, tokens of solidity and grace. Some day there would be a proper place for them.

Mel crossed the kitchen and drew her mother into a sideways hug. "How's it going, Mum?" Edie's fine bones were repeated exactly in Mel's delicate features, her narrow shoulders and slim hips. Her short grey hair clung wetly to the nape of her neck. Mel never failed to think of a fragile bird when she held her mother against her. There was a two-decades difference in their ages and each year was etched on Edie's face. Most of the deep lines and the sadness in her eyes had been added in the last two years.

"Going fine. I have supper started but Ty said we were going to the beach?"

"I think so. It's so hot. Is he getting his things?"

"He's in his room." Edie caught a glimpse of Mel's knees, scabbed with blood and scuffed with dirt. "What happened? You need to clean that."

Mel had a ready answer. "Dumb sandals. I twisted out of one stepping off a curb. I'll clean it." She wouldn't mention Dono's latest intimidation. Edie had enough ammunition for deriding her former son-in-law and didn't need this latest encounter to add to it. She moved towards the bathroom and first aid supplies and called over her shoulder, "Put something together that we can eat at the beach. Maybe sandwiches and veggies. Yogurt, fruit. It doesn't matter." She stood by the sink in the bathroom. With a clean cloth she washed the wounds, thankfully superficial, cleaned with hydrogen peroxide and finished up with an antiseptic ointment.

Ty came running in to see her. "Can I take my mask and flippers?"

"Sure thing. Get a towel too and put it all in your backpack. And your inhaler," she added.

Ty spun out of the room leaving Mel alone in front of the mirror. The heat had deflated her. Her fine blond hair hung in limp stings, her skin shone with a sweaty-sheen. She felt her legs begin to tremble and she leaned against the vanity, supporting herself on her arms. She eased to sitting on the toilet as faint stirrings of nausea rolled across her stomach. She put her head down on her knees and took deep clearing breaths.

Dono's face floated in front of her. She felt his threat as a visceral pain. Why had he started up again? Dono had been an unrelenting menace for several months around her father's arrest and trial, wanting to know where her loyalty stood and don't even think about associating his name with the crime too, whispering that Tyler had enough to live down with a felon for a grandfather. There were veiled threats about living well and living long.

Then he had slackened off. This new intimidation must mean he was riding high again, high and stoned on crystal meth which seemed to make him feel invincible. She could tell that he was arrogantly protecting himself by instilling fear in her. But why now? It had been two years and she hadn't said anything to anybody and never would. She knew in her gut that Dono was as guilty as her father and Nathan Bennett and had escaped charges for lack of evidence. But she had no proof of his guilt nor could she prove his drug use.

She tried to avoid him, didn't want him any where near her and Ty. She had refused support money to distance herself from

Dono's business life and to weaken the hold he had on her. But when Dono insisted on seeing Ty, she knew it wasn't the father role that brought him pleasure. He was letting her know he could control her life, could force her to hand over her most cherished possession, their son.

Mel stood and cupped her hands under cool running water. She splashed her face and neck then patted herself to damp dryness. She drank a glass of water, relishing the coolness. Going to the beach was a good idea. She would be with people, distracted, safe in a group. She could relax and let go of her tension for a few hours. It would be such a relief.

· Chapter 2 ·

~

Joe awoke the next morning disoriented and with muscle cramps in his legs. The single bed that he'd used all his young life didn't leave much room for his six foot frame and the mattress was past its due date. When his eyes focused he saw school pennants and an Edmonton Oilers hockey shirt tacked to the wall above his bed. He touched it—it wasn't too dusty. His mother must actually wash it and put it back on the wall. The bookcase still held sports magazines and other boyhood reading—Moby Dick, Lord of the Rings. There was the trophy he'd won for the highest batting average in his baseball league when he was 15. He hadn't noticed any details of the room when he went to bed last night but he was so familiar with the room, even after 30 years, that he could have sleep-walked through without hitting anything out of place.

Sitting up, his toes sank into the plush mat along side the bed. His mother always had a liking for scatter mats even though it sat over a wall-to-wall rug. He pulled on jeans and a T-shirt and wandered across the hall. The large room that had been his parents' bedroom momentarily startled him with the dining room furniture filling the floor space. The chairs were upturned on the table, like a restaurant declaring it was closed. It hadn't crossed his mind that it had to be *somewhere* other than the downstairs dining room which now held bedroom furniture. He recognized the cream damask drapes with tie-backs that framed the window. Dust balls swirled around the feet of the table and across the hardwood floor.

    A violin case sat on the sideboard. Joe approached it, ran his hand over the dusty surface. His father's violin. The old man used to play. He'd forgotten that. He wasn't half bad, either. Mostly classical pieces but he'd fiddle some high-stepping music for a gathering of friends. His parents had tried to interest Joe in the violin when he was in grade school but sports were more his thing. Yeah, there was a time when there was music in this house but any joy it brought Joe had been snuffed out early by deceit.

    Next to his parents' room was his sister's, Sandra's, old bedroom. It was still girly with pale yellow walls and coral drapes and bedding. A collection of colourful nesting dolls sat on shelves beside the dresser. The Barbie dolls were missing. When he'd left she still had them sitting on the bookcase. Sandra had grown up in his absence. He wondered how Sandra had reacted to the house when she spent that month here when Vera first had the stroke. You'd think she'd at least have sorted and packed her own stuff. Maybe she took the Barbies.

    The whole mood of the upstairs was lost in time, another era. There didn't appear to be any recent updates to the bathroom either. Joe was shaving when the door bell rang. A woman's voice called out to Vera as the door opened. There was bustling in the hallway and another greeting. "Vera? It's Janet. Are you still in bed? I'll be right there."

    Joe let out the breath he didn't know he'd been holding. He was expecting the Home Support Aide but didn't know the morning routine. A worker had arrived last night around nine o'clock and had helped Vera bathe, change and settle into bed. He was relieved by the familiarity the Aide seemed to have with the house and his mother, moving with practiced skill and enthusiasm for her work. Vera was engaged by her kindness and offered weak smiles. Joe had been introduced and Vera, slowly enunciating her words, related some details about Joe and Joe's son in Toronto. They'd disappeared into the bedroom. It left Joe feeling anxious as the reality of his mother's feeble condition took form. When the Aide left, Vera was in bed and a CD player sent out soft sounds of strings that were a Chopin nocturne. It stopped on its own before Joe went to bed.

He sighed with the complexity of the household. He had expected to come and do the needed work but instead he was inside a life he knew nothing about. He hadn't given any thought to his mother's personal needs while she was still at home — until the first time he saw her get up. With halting steps and, balanced with a quad cane and pulling her left leg behind her, she moved towards the bathroom. A sling, applied by her caregiver, supported her paralyzed left arm. He tried not to picture her on her own in the bathroom, underwear twisted around her buttocks — and couldn't imagine how she managed the necessary manoeuvres with clothing and tissue and only one good arm. She didn't ask for help and his relief was palpable.

As last evening had progressed, he'd become increasingly anxious about her continuing needs. She had told him that she would have bedtime help, but what if the Home Support Aide didn't come for some reason? What would he do? What *could* he do? The dining room-as-bedroom had become an invalid's room with creams, sheepskin pads and incontinence products. The air held the essence of oiled skin and toilet needs. Whenever the dining room door was open, Joe kept his eyes forward, avoiding full knowledge of the room. Even in avoidance Joe could see that Vera needed assistance and the thought of helping her to perform personal tasks left him feeling queasy. A son wasn't meant to know his mother in such a personal way.

Sandra should be here. He was the oldest but she was, well ... female. Sure, he knew that it wasn't reasonable for her to come again from Australia, especially when she had been here for the whole month after their mother got out of hospital. She had helped organize the dining room as a bedroom and had set up the caregiver services. Never mind that she was preparing to defend her Ph.D. dissertation. How did that compare with their mother's needs?

Sandra had told him what things were like, how impaired their mother's mobility was. But nothing had prepared him for this. How her body looked collapsed on itself, just like the air had been let out of it. Now, she seemed so organic, the vitality missing. This wasn't supposed to happen at her age. She wasn't even 70 yet. The stressful situation with his father no doubt contributed to the stroke. Now it was left to Sandra and him to make a bad situation better, at least workable. He felt adrift, couldn't see how to hook on to *his* real world. Give him an 870,000 pound 747 to fly any day but spare him from a 100 pound, dependent, old lady. He would help her move and see her well settled. He came here to do home repairs, painting, clearing household debris from the yard in preparation for selling the house. Then he could leave the house that held desperate memories and good riddance to it.

While the caregiver was chatting agreeably to Vera, assisting her to wash and dress, Joe made his way to the kitchen, searched for the coffee and started it dripping, then wandered outside to consider the house repairs.

The house must be 60 years old, Joe thought as he circled the building. The stucco siding had dirtied with time; small cracks could be patched. There were wooden frames and shutters on the windows that needed painting. The porch was in need of some repairs, boards to replace and a coat of paint. He certainly had enough work to keep him busy for two weeks. And that didn't take into account any indoor updating.

He stood at the back of the yard and took a long view of the house. It was his childhood home, the anger-filled framework for his life. Over the years he had overcome the anger and had replaced it with bitterness, a less sharp-edged emotion but one that had crawled into his gut and had never left.

He tried to picture the good times with his mother in her kitchen, cooking for company and fussing with a beautifully laid dining table. But the warm memories wouldn't come. He couldn't find the young Vera; he couldn't get past the medical supplies in the dining room and the wizened body that only half functioned. Vera's diminished state overwhelmed him. He didn't know how to treat her. Most of the time he felt helpless in her presence.

Looking around the yard he tried to shake off the greyness of his thoughts. He found that impossible to do in the enclosed space between the house, garage and back fence. This small area held the bitter secrets. With little effort he could still hear the guttural scrapes, the muffled thump of a soft body connecting with the wall, could feel his nine-year-old confusion and later the memory of his thirteen-year-old loss of innocence.

Joe had never seen his mother acknowledge her husband's clandestine meetings in the back yard. He couldn't remember her ever searching through the window or trembling at the injustice in her life. He had never understood her apparent lack of anger or why she had accepted marginalization in her marriage. Maybe, for a while, she didn't know what was happening so close to her. Maybe she was ignorant by choice. All he knew was that at 17-years-old he couldn't fix it, even with his fists, and in the decades leading up to 47 he hadn't tried.

The early sun beat down on him. He remembered the stillness of the valley summer. Air that was thick to breathe. Being here was oppressive. The air, the house, all pushed down on him. He needed to get to work, get finished and go home. His mother would soon have a new residence and he could junk all this history once and for all.

He focused on the house and tallied the work. Clean the stucco siding, paint the window frames; the eaves had loosened; handrails needed to be stabilized; some planks could be replaced in the porch and some just re-nailed. He should have rented a truck for hauling supplies instead of a car. Obviously his father hadn't done any house repairs in years. He'd be lucky if he could finish here in two weeks.

The detached garage was unlocked and he found the 10-year-old Chrysler sedan covered in dust and crumbling leaves, the license tag two years out of date. Another thing to deal with. The ladder he was looking for was on the floor against the far wall. Maybe he could finish scraping the window frames today.

�

Mel parked her car behind the real estate office, gathered her purse over her shoulder and settled the loose cotton sundress around her knees. She plucked a sweater from the back seat knowing she would need it when the frigid air conditioning her boss required reached full force. As she unlocked the back door she could already feel tendrils of cloying heat wrap around her neck. The 68-degree air always provided a welcome blast of cool relief after doing errands out of the office, but sitting at her desk working on the computer and answering the phone kept her on the brink of shivers.

She set the coffee maker and activated the switchboard console. She had worked for Nicols Realty for three years. Tyler was just four-years-old at the time she started. By then, Mel knew enough about Dono's private life to know she would leave him. She couldn't stay married to someone who used drugs, who was emotionally unstable and unpredictable.

The first time she recognized his drug use was at a party. Scott Nicols had commented about Dono not looking well. Mel had watched him go into a bathroom irritable and come out the life of the party. Then she knew. She knew his flares of temper followed by apologies and gifts were due to drugs. She knew his drive to make money was for drugs. When Dono heard the news of her job he had exploded in injured pride and loss of spousal control. While Dono's threats rang loudly in the air, she gave him an ultimatum. Me or drugs. Get off or get out.

Things improved enough that she thought he had his problem under control. She rode a roller-coaster of emotions for a couple more years then knew she had to leave. With her mother a willing babysitter, this job was a life-saver.

Scott breezed through the front door at exactly nine o'clock, a handful of mail in his grasp. Dressed in a golf shirt and khakis, he looked cool and energetic. His extra bulk made it difficult for him to stay that way for long and the controlled low air temperature was his way of coping.

"'Morning, Mel."

"Hi, Scott. Another scorcher, eh?"

"Yeah. You can start thanking me for the air conditioning any time now," Scott teased.

Mel smiled and inclined her head in formal homage. "Consider yourself thanked," she said.

Scott handed over the mail. "I caught the postie on the way in."

Mel began opening and sorting as Scott headed for his office. "Hey, Scott!" she called. "It's come. The package from the Commerce Department at UBC." She tore at the manila envelope from the university and slid the contents onto the desk. Scott came back to look over her shoulder.

"Hey, this is great," he said.

Mel was looking at the first lesson of the *Residential Trading*

Services Licensing Course which would enable her to become a real estate agent. She was upgrading her skills with this online course through the University of British Columbia and would finish it is less than a year. Scott had promised her a position as an agent in his office. It was going to mean the end of scrimping and denying Tyler some of the activities he wanted. With any luck the baby boomers would keep trading houses into retirement and old age and she would have the money to help Tyler through college.

"Yeah, really great," she enthused.

The phone's ring interrupted them. As Mel took the call, the door opened and Dono entered the office, his step eager and full of confidence. The silky sheen of his shirt proclaimed its high price tag. The drape and crease of his trousers said designer label. Because of the arrogance of his walk, his look just missed being classy.

"'Morning, Scott. How's it going?" Dono extended his hand. Scott's grip was slow and puzzled.

"What can I do for you, Donovan?" This was a first, Mel's ex-husband walking into their office.

Dono glanced at Mel, clearly relishing her surprise. Mel turned away from them, seemingly absorbed by the particulars of the call.

"What you can do for me is maybe sell me a commercial building. The office I'm in is too big for just me and, besides, it's a rental. Time maybe to own instead. There's that small building on Baker Street that you have advertised."

"Really?" The response was reluctant. He knew just enough about Mel's former husband to be wary. He hesitated a moment then invited Dono into his office to talk further.

Mel's call ended and her eyes followed the men down the hallway. She was more than startled at Dono showing up here. He hadn't been in the office more than three times during their marriage. She felt chilled and reached for her sweater. More calls and computer work filled the next 20 minutes until Dono and Scott emerged from the office.

"Mel, I'm taking Donovan over to that property on Baker Street. I have an appointment here around 10:30. Be back before then."

Mel nodded and watched as the men walked to the parking lot knowing Scott would tell her later just what was going on.

～

Joe took a break from scraping paint and asked his mother for the car keys and, with searching, she came up with them in a kitchen drawer. He walked around the car, examining its finish and couldn't find any flaws. When he turned the ignition the cylinders purred to life. He backed it into the driveway and let it run for a while. It was a large luxury car and might be hard to sell but the engine sounded fine.

Back in the kitchen and ready for food, he found his mother in the living room watching TV. He poked his head around the doorway. "Mom, do you want a sandwich?"

She shook her head no. She pointed to the kitchen. "In the fridge," she said. When Joe checked, a sandwich was ready under plastic wrap. He went to the doorway again. "Where did that come from?" he asked.

"Janet. She makes them."

Joe raised his eyebrows in question.

"Yeah. Every day." She smiled her lopsided smile as if this was a joke on him.

"Great." Joe chuckled. "Do you want it now?"

Vera shook her head emphatically.

He made himself a sandwich, piled on layers of ham, cheese and pickles. He took a cold beer from the fridge and went to sit with his mother in the living room.

Joe watched Vera's concentration on the television. Her paralyzed arm was weighing down a book of crossword puzzles and with her other hand she was penciling in answers. Once in a while she would raise her head to follow the TV program. He was dismayed at how content she seemed. She was coping, if you could call it that. He knew he wouldn't in similar circumstances. Needing help to function in the most elementary ways wasn't really coping, was it?

The last time he had seen her was in Vancouver four months ago. He had an extended overnight and she came in by bus to visit with him. She had been energetic and happy, pleased to be squired around by her pilot son and introduced to other crew members. He was lucky in a way. As a commercial pilot he could see her quite frequently, when Vancouver was part of his scheduled runs. He'd missed a lot of years with her, avoiding his father and the home town. He'd been hard-lined about never setting foot in his father's house again after he left. He and his ex-wife, Karen, had fought bitterly about this decision, he adamant that the passage of years does not nullify unforgivable behaviour, she arguing that he was neglecting his mother and causing her to suffer without justification. Visits had mostly happened when Vera travelled to Toronto when his son, Devon, was small. Now that Devon lived with his mother it wasn't as easy. But Joe had been seeing her more often on the west coast in these last two years of his father's absence.

"Mom," he said. Vera jerked her head around, startled at his voice, as if she'd forgotten he was there.

"If I went out to dinner tonight, would you be okay?"

She looked at him as if he'd asked her if the sky was blue, took a minute to answer. "Yes. I've been okay for many years now." She turned away briefly then looked at him again.

Joe blushed at the intended rebuke. She looked at her son. "I'll be fine," she slurred. "Meals-On-Wheels tonight. Then, Home

Support." She turned back to the television.

"Okay." His voice was soft, chastised.

"Do you remember Scott Nicols?" he asked. She nodded. "Sure you do. You mentioned him. I saw him yesterday and he invited me to their cottage for a barbeque. I'll leave around five." She nodded again.

"I... I go to the home to see Nathan today. Always on Thursday."

"You go...?"

"Yeah, on the speshal bus." Vera's words were distorted.

"Special bus?" Joe was confused and couldn't picture his mother traveling by bus anywhere.

"Yeah. They come at three." She pointed to the clock. "Two hours."

Vera on a bus? Joe turned this over in his mind for a minute, but knew the conclusion he had to reach, knew what was expected.

"I guess I could take you instead," he said.

Vera looked closely at him. "Yeah, I guess you could." She fumbled with a note pad. "Phone number of bus. Call them and say I don't need them."

Joe made the call then told Vera he would work outside a while longer. This was happening too soon. He didn't want to see his father. He wasn't prepared for a confrontation. Anxiety and anger fuelled his work. He found he was scraping the wood frames with fast, deep strokes. Maybe he wouldn't have to see him, just drop his mother and go find a coffee. He scraped faster. He wondered what a deliberate avoidance of his father would do to his mother. Could it set her health back somehow?

He sighed in confusion. He thought his role as handyman would cover everything he had to do. Now his role as son got stepped up a notch. He decided to stay outside longer where he knew who he was and what to do.

Time passed too quickly. Before he had worked out an alternate plan, he found himself helping his mother into the car and driving towards the care facility, a short fifteen minute trip.

As they approached the entrance to the building, the door swung open as if by magic. Vera hobbled through the doorway with her cane and made a straight line for the elevator.

"Hi, Vera. I saw you coming so opened the door from this side." The woman was in her fifties with a short, round stature. Her close-cropped grey hair required no fussing in the morning and her choice of an Hawiian-print shift displayed her lack of interest in style. Her face beamed with welcome.

She extended her hand to Joe. "Hi, I'm Catherine. Clerk-receptionist."

Joe shook her hand, his eyes taking in the soothing colours in the décor and the fresh flowers on the desk.

"Joe," he said. "Vera's son."

"Then I guess you're Nathan's too." Catherine smiled brightly. Vera seemed unable to stop her forward motion and was thumping towards the elevator.

Joe gave a curt nod.

"She's always anxious to see Nathan," she confided in a quiet aside. "He's looking good today, Vera," she called. Then to Joe, "Enjoy your visit."

The elevator opened onto a reception area. A long-term care aide and nurse were conferring at the desk. Vera voiced a weak hello and both turned to greet her.

"Vera! So nice to see you today." Her name tag announced that she was Claire. "Nathan's waiting in his room. If you didn't come every Thursday we'd have to find some other reason to fuss over him." Claire beamed.

Claire pressed numbers on a keypad and opened the door to a long corridor with numbered doors on each side. The reality of a locked unit shocked Joe, as much because it was treated with casualness by the staff. Vera continued walking, unconcerned and concentrating on her destination.

There were obvious attempts at brightness with quilted wall hangings adding colour and texture to the beige corridor. Doors to rooms announced their occupants as 'Doris', 'Edgar', 'Clarence', 'Muriel'. On each door, under the name, was a picture of a young person. They were obviously old pictures that had been enlarged. Joe couldn't see the point.

Several people walked in the hallway. One frail lady with wispy white hair wore a pink chenille housecoat and a red scarf, and mitts. She hummed to herself as she dusted the hand rails along the wall with her mittens. A tall, gangly man in a tweed suit coat stood in the middle of the hallway clapping his hands softly to some silent rhythm. Vera kept moving and stopped in front of number twelve. Joe was behind her. Riveted by the bizarre sights around him, he bumped into Vera's back and came to an abrupt halt.

Nathan's door had his name above a picture that Joe remembered from his childhood. His father had caught a fish and was holding it towards the camera. A huge smile creased his face. Joe thought his father must have been about 35-years-old then.

Nathan was seated in an easy chair. No longer the tall, robust man, with dark wavy hair and the broad shoulders that Joe remembered and had inherited. Nathan had had a quick smile and an engaging charm that caused women to turn and look when he entered a room. Men looked as well, usually to keep track of their wives.

Now Nathan seemed small in the large chair. He was shrivelled with bony angles poking through his shirt. His grey hair had thinned and had comb tracks slicing front to back. Hair curled around his shirt collar. He wore navy chinos that were faded from harsh commercial washing. A radio played classical music in the background.

Vera clumped into the room with her quad cane, Joe behind her, and Nathan looked up at them. He could have been looking at a rock with as much interest. He looked away, seemingly attracted by a bird outside. Vera sat beside him and took his hand. He pulled away, startled by the touch. When she started to talk, Nathan was attracted to the buttons on her dress and touched each of them tentatively. He tapped the buttons absently until he was distracted by the bird again. His attention rested there for a moment.

Vera began chatting to him, slurred words running together. She produced a package of gummie bears from her purse. She offered Nathan one and he sucked on it intently. She said the word Joe and indicated their son. Nathan stared without recognition. Nathan looked at Vera again. "Mary," he said. "Mary. Where's Vera?"

Vera looked up at Joe. "He thinks... my mother." Her eyes teared and her face crumpled. "Sometimes he says Vera."

Joe didn't speak. He swallowed the bile that rose in his throat. He was stunned at the dramatic change in his father. Nathan had been loudly in charge in his home and had been a compelling force in the community. The last time Joe had seen his father, Nathan was bloodied around the nose and lips, shouting in anger and fear at his son. Joe had wiped his own bloody hands on his pants and had turned away from Nathan and his home for the next three decades.

Joe had anticipated a confrontation with the old man, with enough blame and accusation spewing out to cover everyone in the family. That was the man he remembered. Instead, Nathan was a shell of a human who didn't appear to know who Joe was or even that he was there. The balding grey-haired man with age spots over his hands and forehead looked like time had sucked the life force out of him.

Joe stood back from them and watched the pathetic scene.

Gwen Enquist

The Twilight-Zone behaviour of the people in the hall had put him on edge. The locked ward was shocking in its implications. The pitiful scene between his parents made him feel like throwing up. He watched his mother struggling by sheer will to pull Nathan back into the world of remembering. She was explaining to Nathan that she was Vera, not Mary. Nathan looked through her with empty eyes and repeated Mary, Mary. Sometimes he looked at Joe and said Will.

A caregiver appeared at the door with a glass of juice for Nathan. Vera put her good hand over Nathan's to help guide the glass to his mouth. He drank thirstily.

Joe felt trapped. The locked doors and key pad codes that had startled him at first now made him claustrophobic. He didn't know how to act. He moved to the window and was silent. He hated this.

Finally, Vera indicated that they should go. She said goodbye to Nathan and assured him that she would be back. She kissed his cheek. Nathan pulled back, startled and continued to stare at her.

When they reached the outdoors, Joe breathed deeply and stretched to his full height, grateful for the open space. The fact that Nathan had escaped a prison with bars was of no consequence. He had entered a prison of even greater limitations, one without referents to self or to life-affirming humanity.

Did he deserve it? Did anyone? The poor bugger, Joe thought. He thought I was his brother, Will. Will, dead 32 years ago.

He couldn't wait to get Vera to the house and leave again. An evening at the lake with Scott couldn't happen at a better time.

☙

Scott, dressed in swim trunks and with an oversized-towel draped around his shoulders, walked from the lake up the gently rolling grass to his deck. He was puffing by the time he climbed the slope.

His wife, Marion, stepped onto the deck from the kitchen and called to him. "Hey, Scott. We've got company and a swimming partner for you."

Mel, with Tyler and Edie following behind her, appeared around the corner of the cedar-shake cottage. Ty waved energetically with his snorkel. "Hi, Scott. You're not finished are you? I've got my flippers and everything." He bounded down the expanse of lawn and caught Scott by the arm. "Let's go. I want to swim between your legs. You're the goalpost, remember?"

Scott looked at the women and shrugged a what-can-I-do shrug and took Tyler's hand. Ty tugged at Scott to move faster as they made their way back to the water.

"Scott's such a softie," Mel commented.

Marion chuckled. "If a little kid just bats his eyes and looks doleful, Scott would give him the world." She had a stocky frame and short grey hair in a 'wash and wear' cut. Her country-casual clothing suited their relaxed lifestyle

"You're a lucky woman, Marion," Mel said sincerely. Marion already knew that. She and Scott walked the same walk and talked the same talk. To an observer their life together appeared seamless and, if asked, they would tell you that it was. She complemented Scott's easy friendliness with her own welcoming attitude. They each had the knack of making everyone feel like a friend.

"I know." She touched Mel's arm and looked at her. "Scott told me Dono was in the office today. That could make you uneasy."

"It did, for a few minutes. Then I thought, 'Dono and I live in the same town and I have to deal.' But you're right. It's not easy."

"What about a beer or wine? Wind down from the day," Marion offered.

"Sure. A beer would be cooling."

Marion turned to Edie. "And Edie? What can I get you?"

Edie turned from studying her grandson swimming around Scott's legs. "Some white wine with some 7-Up?"

33

"Sure. I'll be right back."

Mel and Edie seated themselves in deck chairs, turning towards the water each time they heard Ty shriek. Tyler was keeping Scott fully occupied as a goalpost and when Ty wanted to climb on Scott's shoulders and jump off, Scott grabbed him instead and tossed him over his back. The splashing and laughter were the background as more people started arriving.

"Hey, Marion." Neil Heslop rounded the corner of the deck, his wife Elaine beside him. Elaine carried a salad bowl of greens covered in plastic wrap.

"Hi, you guys. Come on up." Marion relieved Elaine of the bowl and took it inside. The couple was just pulling up chairs when a tall, thin man and a short, chubby woman appeared at the corner.

"Hey, are we late?" Marco Di Silva greeted Neil and Elaine. "Hi, Mel. Great to see you. And Edie. Hi." Both Marco and his wife, Gina, hugged Mel and her mother. Gina took her dessert plate into the cottage.

Marion carried a tray to the deck with several beers, two open bottles of wine and glasses. While everyone was finding their drinks, Scott and Ty came up the lawn to the deck. Ty was wheezing and Scott had wrapped a large towel around the small shoulders. You could hear an audible rasp with each breath. Scott scooped him up into his arms.

"Sorry, Mel. I guess we got carried away. He's breathing pretty heavy." Scott lifted Ty up the steps of the deck and settled him in a chair. Mel ran her hand over Ty's head, as much caress as assessment of his distress. "I'll get his inhaler," she said.

She went into the house just as Joe turned the corner of the building. Scott called hello and Joe was immediately welcomed by people he hadn't seen in 30 years. Neil and Marco, Scott and Joe. The Four Caballeros of Sardis High. Joe shook his head in wonder and smiled at them all being here together.

Scott was sitting beside Ty holding his hand. "This is our friend, Ty." He said, introducing Joe. "He's having a little problem right now but his mother will fix him up right away." He looked up as Mel returned. "Won't you, Mel? He'll be like new in a few minutes."

Mel handed the inhaler to Ty and guided him in using it. The routine was familiar and finished quickly. Scott got up and gave Mel his chair.

"He'll be fine in a few minutes," she said. Mel caressed Ty's hair and watched him breathe. Ty's chest muscles began to relax and his breathing became easier.

Joe leaned against the deck railing watching Mel care for Ty. She was soothing and gentle as she enfolded Ty in a cocoon of parental safety. It stirred him in ways that he had forgotten, touching a centre where protective instincts lay dormant. He watched Mel safeguarding her child and realized that he used to care that much too, back when family life with Karen and Devon was good. He hadn't been around that depth of caring for too many years to count. It touched a chord of longing in him, an ache for tenderness. What had happened to that capacity in him to give and receive soft emotions? Had it been destroyed or just worn down, abraded by too much discord?

Neil was talking to him, handing him a beer, introducing his wife into the conversation. Neil was saying what at hole it left in their lives when Joe left so suddenly.

"Man. One day you were there and the next you were gone." Neil took a pull on his beer.

Joe glanced at Marco, wondering how sharp his memory was for events of 30 years ago. He drew his attention back to Neil and raised his beer in salute. "That's the way it is when the recruiter has your number," Joe grinned. "Things happen fast."

"Yeah, you lucky dog, you learned to fly," Neil drank deeply again. "You had guts enough to try the great unknown. I'll bet you saw something of the world too."

35

"Yeah. I went a few places. I was in the Gaza as part of the U.N. forces. And Bosnia. None of it's fun, Neil."

"I know, sure. But you had an adventure. I'm still working on the courage for mine. Eh, Elaine?" He pulled his wife into a loose embrace.

Elaine acknowledged him with a toss of her head. "We'll get there, Neil. It'll be *our* adventure." She turned to Joe. "We got our Canadian Yachting Association Certification a few years ago. Now we're looking for a catamaran that is ocean-worthy. We want to sail to Australia."

As Elaine filled everyone in on the progress of their search for a suitable boat, Joe focused again on Mel who was bending over Ty, her hair draping his face like a shield and glinting with coppery sun streaks. It was such an honest moment that shattered when Mel raised her head and noticed Joe. Her eyes widened in surprise. He lifted his beer in greeting, allowing a smile to test her reaction. She hesitated a second then shrugged her shoulders as if it didn't matter. Ty claimed her attention again by asking for a drink. He was recovered enough to go into the cottage with Mel. The capsule of warmth evaporated leaving Joe to wonder if Mel would be eternally ungracious.

Soon the aroma and sizzle of barbequed steaks drifted in the still evening air. Large bowls of colourful salads weighted the table. Scott announced the steaks to be perfect and everyone better come get them before he took *his* share. Laughter and light-hearted teasing bounced from person to person, first targeting Scott and then Marco. It was Neil who uttered the first do-you-remember.

"Joe, do you remember the tree fort we had on the back lot? The boys-only fort? That summer we stayed here with Scott so much? Man, that was fun. We spent days with hammers and scrap wood and actually got a structure together that didn't collapse the first time we all stood on it."

"And, Neil, you were the one who nearly ruined it all when you said you thought girls should be allowed into it too," Scott added.

"Well, hell, I was precocious."

"Joe, do you remember the day you rescued Mel when she drifted out too far on the rubber tube?' Scott asked.

Joe looked over at Mel whose face washed with confusion, then embarrassment.

"No, I don't. What happened?" he asked.

Scott looked at Mel, expecting her to jump in with the memory. Her mouth opened slightly but stopped there.

"Her whole family had come out for the afternoon," Scott said. "We were all swimming and, you know how we were supposed to watch the younger kids? Well, of course, we didn't and there was Mel floating half way across the lake. Do you remember, Mel?"

Mel blushed. "I remember not being the least bit bothered about being out that far. Thought it was kind of a joke on everyone, getting away like that."

"Well, it was Joe who started up the boat and went to pull you back in."

Joe looked at Mel who averted her eyes. Joe closed his eyes for second, trying to bring the memory back.

"I'm afraid I don't remember that," Joe said.

"Well," said Marco, "none of us was interested in girls back then. Except Neil." Everyone laughed.

"I remember the time Scott's father tried to trick us into painting this cottage for him," Joe said. "Told us he was getting it ready for a home improvement competition and we could help him win." Joe smiled and shook his head at the thought.

"Yeah," Scott laughed. "He almost had us believing we could win a new boat and outboard."

"And he took us to see the boat and everything. Too bad Mr. Eccles, the dealer, told us Mr. Nicols was ready to buy it anyway.

I wish I had his imagination and maybe I could come up with something to get you guys to help me paint my mother's house?"

"Have you got quite a bit to do there?" Scott asked.

"More than I bargained on. It hasn't had much attention for a few years."

A momentary quiet settled over the group. Marco cleared his throat. "Well, speaking for myself, I'd rather sit in a boat and drink beer any day than paint a house." This was followed by general laughter at Marco who hired out every kind of household repair. "But I do know someone who can help you. He does odd jobs and he's good at it. If you need him let me know."

"Great. Maybe I'll decide to use him," Joe replied.

Mel began stirring and said it was time to get Ty home before he fell asleep and before mosquitoes ate her totally. Edie stood too, picking up towels as she went into the cottage. Marion got up to see them off.

Marco asked Joe if he had anything happening on Wednesday afternoon. "I'm taking some time to fish," he smiled. "Would you like to come? Have you got the time?"

"Hey, that'd be great," Joe said. "What about tackle?"

"I've got lots," he said. He gave Joe his address and they arranged a time.

The other guests soon followed and, with Marion tidying the kitchen, Scott poured himself and Joe a brandy. They were alone on the porch.

"It was great being here again," Joe said. "Do you stay out here all summer?"

"As much as we can. Especially with weather like this."

"And your kids?"

"They're with their grandparents in Calgary. For the Stampede."

"Lucky kids. Summer at the lake and grandparents that can entertain them too." Joe paused. "Do you think they have as much fun here as we did?"

"It's a bit different. The toys are bigger, more expensive," Scott chuckled. "But, you know, I try with them. We don't have a TV here, no electronic toys. For a few days they sulk about not having their Game-Boy or iPods or something. Then they settle in. I make sure they get involved in building stuff and fishing. We build a raft every year. Then we have a launching party. Invite all the friends and hope it floats." He laughed again. "Last year they got the raft out deep enough to be over their heads. It was quite an elaborate one with a diving tower on one side. Well, the damn thing toppled over with that lop-sided weight and started sinking. They could swim, of course. So everybody on shore was either laughing or cheering for them."

"Those are great memories. Fun stuff," Joe said. Each sat quietly for a few moments, sipping their drinks.

Joe broke the silence. "I wish I could have remembered rescuing Mel Compton." He paused. "I saw her yesterday. In a parking lot. She'd stumbled. Some guy pointed a finger at her like it was a gun. Scared her, I guess. She skinned her knees. I wanted to help…but she…blew me off. Almost rude when she learned who I was."

"Mel's been hurting pretty bad ever since her father's conviction. She left her husband, Donovan Harris, and her mother moved in with her. I'll bet it was Dono who scared her. That sounds like his style. Edie, that's Mel's mother, didn't have any money with the Crown freezing all of Owen's accounts. As far as I know they're still frozen. Lots of litigation pending from people who lost money."

"So Owen was charged with…what? Embezzlement?"

"That and Conspiracy to Defraud and Fraud. He was convicted on all charges."

"My mother hasn't been clear on my father's part in it. Just that he couldn't stand trial. What do you know, Scott?"

Scott studied Joe's face then shrugged, giving in to the

inevitable. "As far as the authorities know, he and Owen had a scam going in which your father would get his clients all kinds of tax deductions that skirted the edge of legal, and sometimes didn't even try to make it legal. Just tried to see how far he could go. Then he'd back track if need be, admit a mistake, so sorry, and pay up. But the biggest problem was that these people liked him. He was always an affable guy and he won their confidence and friendship, and, because he did such a good job of saving on the taxes, they trusted him."

"That just sounds like he was riding the fence and seeing how long it took to fall off," Joe commented. He sipped his drink and considered the implications. Then Scott broke in.

"But that's just part of it. It seems your father gained people's confidence and then recommended that they invest money through Owen. He was an investment and securities advisor." Scott waited a minute till Joe could get the picture. "And then they used that money for their own investments. And, I've heard, they were quite successful, giving back a profit as well as taking one themselves."

"How did they get caught? How did it fall apart?"

"It was your father." Scott waited a beat. "This was when his illness became noticeable. He started losing track of accounts, posting entries wrong, mixing one account with another. Or simply forgetting to do it. People started to talk, get worried. Then a couple of them moved their accounts to another company. That's when the discrepancies showed up and everything collapsed."

Both men were silent for a while, sat watching the lake, the inky darkness shot with a streak of silver from the quarter moon.

"Remember how we used to row out along the moonbeams? See how far we could go before it got dark?" Joe said.

Scott could see that the subject had changed. "They really were the best times, weren't they?"

"Absolutely the best. Thanks for this evening, Scott." Joe said softly.

"Well, I'll show you the way to end a great evening. Lay your head back in the chair."

Scott got up turned off the porch lights to extinguish the temporal world. The men lay back in the chairs and each slid into a comfortable slouch. The dense blackness of the rural night closed around them. The moon trailed a path across the lake, stars blinked in a velvet sky and crickets sang their mating sounds. The two friends nursed their drinks and listened to the night.

· Chapter 3 ·

☙

Mel was multi-tasking at the computer and telephone consol. The boom in the real estate market not only kept her busy but also hopeful about her own future. The phone never stopped ringing and people came through the office doors in a steady stream, looking for property.

It took her a minute to look up before she saw Dono standing at the desk, grinning at her.

"Aren't you the busy little beaver? So glad to see it, Mel. Then maybe you won't miss Ty when I take him this weekend."

Mel froze in her chair and stared at Dono. Even with him grinning she could see he was serious. It was just like him to phrase it like it could mean keeping Ty forever. Even though she knew that Ty wouldn't fit Dono's lifestyle, that he would never want to take care of a child on a permanent basis, it made her throat clog with fear.

"And if I have other plans for us this weekend?" It was a weak challenge but she couldn't just acquiesce without some protest, however feeble.

"Mel…," Dono said with feigned patience edged with sarcasm, "we both know you'll have Ty ready for me to pick up Friday night." He grinned again. "Just make sure he's packed by seven o'clock. We're going to a cottage so pack his swimming gear."

Dono turned away and headed for the door.

Mel called out to him. "Dono. I'll pack his medication but I'll go over it with you before you take off on Friday."

"You think I don't know what to do? You're not the only parent, Mel." He slammed the door behind him.

Mel sank into her chair. She felt a presence behind her and turned to see Scott standing at her shoulder.

"What was that about, Mel?"

"Just Dono showing his muscles. He wants Ty this weekend."

"He seemed kind of hostile. Is he always like that?"

"Lately, yes. I don't know what's got into him." Mel swallowed dryly. "He…he's been intimidating lately. Like he has to grind me into the ground or something."

"Well, I don't want to pry or anything … but if you're having problems … can I help or is it the kind of problem a lawyer can deal with?"

"I don't know yet. But thanks. As long as it doesn't affect Ty … I'll be fine." She smiled up at Scott, displaying a strength she didn't feel. Scott squeezed her shoulder before turning back to his office.

Mel let out her breath. She felt like she was treading on quicksand with Dono. She could sink at anytime, or Dono could push her under. Why now? What's happened to make him feel threatened by her? She hadn't told authorities anything after being questioned over and over again. Because Dono was a friend and business associate of her father's it was believed that he was part of the embezzlement scheme. She had told them he had a motive, money for drugs, but Dono didn't share an office with Owen and they couldn't move on suspicions only. There had been nothing to justify a search warrant.

She could stand up to Dono if she had to. She clutched her arms around herself. At least, she thought she could. Just let him leave Ty alone. If Dono ever harmed him she would have him in court so fast he wouldn't have time to think up his next intimidation.

❧

By the middle of the next week Joe had all the window frames scraped and ready for painting. He had secured and cleaned the gutters, nailed some boards down on the porch and needed to find a truck to buy replacement lumber. Scott told him that Marco had a truck and would probably loan it for that job. Marco readily agreed, said Joe could pick the truck up at his work and return it there. He didn't need it for the afternoon.

When he returned the truck, Marco suggested Joe come to the baseball field that night. Gina and 16-year-old Jenna, were playing baseball — their games were back to back and started at 6pm. They always made a picnic out of it. Joe said he'd be there.

The playing field was busy with four baseball diamonds throughout the huge park area. Jenna was playing when Joe arrived and Gina was waiting for her own team. "We play over in that corner," she said, indicating the west side of the field. Marco was using a portable gas barbeque to cook hot dogs and there were raw vegetables and dip for a nod to good nutrition.

"Step up here, Joe, this dog has your name on it," Marco said.

Joe thought this was the best part of summer — relaxing on the warm grass with friends and grilled food.

"I could get used to this summer living," Joe said. "It's harder to find in Toronto."

"How hard?" Gina asked.

"You either have to travel out of the city or find a beach on the lake with thousands of other people." Joe looked around. "This is better," he grinned.

Marco kept his eye on Jenna's play and cheered her on. "She's got a great arm, hasn't she?" he said to no one in particular. Angela was still eating hot dogs and watching a pick-up soccer game along the fenced boundary of the park. Players were gathering around Gina, organizing their line-up. Mel appeared, seemingly out of no where, and stopped still when she saw Joe. Tyler was hanging onto her hand.

Joe uttered, "Hi, Mel," and continued talking to Marco. Mel nodded. She indicated that Tyler should go and sit with Marco's nine-year-old, Angela.

"Mel Compton doesn't seem to want to know me," Joe said.

Marco shrugged. "She's changed some since her divorce — and since her father went to prison. It's like she's carrying the guilt but still wants everyone to know she's not part of it."

"It's really nothing to do with me," Joe said. "Our fathers had their own lives and I had mine."

"Mel seems to feel that way too but lives with it daily. She's distancing herself from Owen and Dono by withdrawing from that part of the family."

"I guess it's as good a coping technique as any," Joe said. He'd used avoidance. Sounds like the same thing to him.

Gina's and Mel's team hit the field. Joe watched Mel, her short curls bobbing through the opening in her baseball cap. She was crouched in an infielder stance, slim muscular legs taut with expectation. Marco cheered from the sidelines. Joe caught the enthusiasm and clapped for good plays. Mel was outstanding, catching a fly ball that put the two players on base out. Joe could see that she was keeping Tyler's whereabouts on her radar screen. He admired her for her devotion to Tyler but also that she made time for her own interests.

"Uh, Joe?"

"Yeah, sorry, my mind was wandering."

"I can see the direction it's wandering in," Marco grinned.

"Not a bad direction at that," Joe said.

"So ... tomorrow. I'm taking the afternoon off. I've got flex time and want to do some fishing. Are you up for it?"

"Sure," Joe said. "What time?"

They made their arrangements. Joe headed back to Vera's. Once inside he heard the strains of a Mozart melody coming from Vera's bedroom. Joe smiled. It was a nice way to settle for the night.

Marco's invitation to go fishing was great, timely, even if the sun beat down relentlessly in the afternoons. Joe painted in the relative coolness of the morning then resting in the afternoon followed by more work in the evening. Vera usually napped after lunch so today he would leave her alone to rest without him having to tip-toe around the house and catch the back door before it banged whenever he sat on the porch with a beer.

He was impressed with Marco's house and land. The yard stretched deeply in back to a stand of fir trees that were probably the property line. The house was set well back from the road, a two-storied traditional façade, brick work along the foundation and cedar siding to the roof line. The front door was flanked by white columns that added a strong presence to the entrance. The boat on a trailer hooked to the truck was in the driveway at the back of the house. Marco was putting gear in the boat. Joe added his small cooler of beer. Gina came to the door with Angela at her side.

"Catch a big salmon, Daddy," Angela said.

"And clean it before you hand it over," Gina teased.

"Aye, aye, captains." Marco mock saluted then stepped up to Gina for a quick kiss. "See you later." He blew a kiss to Angela.

Joe looked on with envy.

Joe liked Marco's boat as soon as he saw it. It was an 18-foot fibre-glass hull with a 125-horse motor. "Nice set-up," Joe said. Soon Marco was refreshing Joe on how to launch a boat and they were putting lines out.

Marco looked with pleasure at his boat. "I always wanted a boat. Remember how I used to say I was going to have one." Joe nodded. "I didn't wait long. Bought it the first chance I had."

"Looks like a great unit," Joe said.

"Could be bigger, flashier. But all I care about is being able to fish or the kids being able to water-ski. This one works." He paused. "Okay. Let's slaughter fish," he grinned.

They trolled slowly until they found a flock of sea gulls feeding on herring. Then Marco speeded a bit to buck-tail through the herring swirls. Joe quickly had a bite. He let the line run and reeled in when the fish rested. The thrill of bringing in a catch was still there. Marco netted it with a flourish.

"What do you think? About a five-pounder?" Joe looked at the fish then at his friend.

"I'd say so. It's a keeper for sure." They reset their lines and moved through the herring again. Marco's line was hit this time and brought in a smaller version of Joe's fish. It was below the legal limit and they threw it back. By this time the herring had moved on and they couldn't see any more schools swirling around them.

"Let's just troll for a while," Marco said.

They each settled back against the vinyl seats. Marco glanced over at Joe. "So, how does it feel? Being back?"

Joe hesitated. "You know how it was when I left?" Marco nodded. He'd helped keep Joe in food and shelter until they finished their last two weeks of school. Joe refused to go home. He saw his mother twice to reassure her he was alright. Vera just gulped tears when Joe wouldn't stay. When Joe had come back to Marco's house bloody and dirty, Joe had told him there had been a fight and he was never going home again. During those last two weeks before he left, Joe spent weekends at Marco's house and had hidden out at Scott's family cottage during the week. He'd slept on the porch, washed in the lake, used their outhouse and finished his exams. Marco was the only person who knew where he was and the truth about the fight.

"Being back hurts almost as much as 30 years ago." He looked at Marco who nodded as if wanting him to continue. Joe measured his words. "My mother acts like nothing happened. Just goes on with her life, limited as it now is, and doesn't ask anything." He paused and ordered his thoughts. "I went to see Nathan because Mom was going and because I felt sort of pressured into it. She didn't say anything but I felt the expectation. Like when your parents don't ask you to do something, just say it's up to you, but you know all along if you don't you'll be in their bad books."

'I guess they never stop being your parents no matter how old you are," Marco said with a rueful grin.

"Well, Nathan has stopped being my father." Joe said. Marco nodded, misunderstanding. "Not because of the fight," Joe said, "but because he thinks I'm his brother."

"What …?"

"He has dementia so bad he doesn't even know me. Here I was dreading having to see him and now he doesn't know me."

"Well … that makes it easier, in a way, doesn't it?"

Joe was thoughtful. He shrugged his shoulders. "I guess." He waited a beat. "Does that mean the last 30 years I've been angry and sure of myself and now it's just vanished? Does that event just vanish like it never happened?"

"Not for you," Marco said. "The event still happened but the fallout is different now."

Joe smirked. "If a tree falls in the forest and nobody's there does it make a sound?"

"Is that what it feels like?"

"Yeah, sort of. It was a big event and I expected to hear a roar and it didn't happen."

"So what does that mean?"

"I guess it means I get to absorb all of the sound waves."

They sat in silence for a while then decided the bite was over. Joe gave Marco the fish for Angela.

At home, Vera had eaten and Joe could see where she had tried to clean the food mess. Joe found a cloth and finished the job. The air had cooled so he changed his clothes and was soon up a ladder again with a paint can in hand.

Joe heard the house phone ringing with its protracted noise. Since his mother couldn't answer it anymore, the ringing went on and on. Surely, anybody close to her knew not to phone, although this limitation to her movements hadn't occurred to him too fast either. Here he was on a ladder two stories up the side of the house and no way to get to the phone in the kitchen before the caller gave up. Only minutes later his cell phone rang and rang, insisting on a response, but he couldn't answer it either. With a paint brush in one hand and balancing a bucket of paint with the other, he would plan his return to ground level by the work in progress, not someone's idea of an urgent message.

He was irritable and he knew it. His afternoon's pleasure in the boat hadn't carried through to evening. It was the ever present heat and the anger the house generated. The more he scraped and painted the more anger at his father swirled around and found a foothold in the neglected house. The thought that his father had scammed a lot of money from people but somehow hadn't seen the necessity of maintenance work on the house was galling. If Nathan was making such a success of profitting from embezzled money, why didn't he spend some on his house? What was with the lack of attention to the ordinary requirements of home ownership? Most criminals would spend on luxuries, or at least quality consumer goods. But there was no evidence that Nathan had "enjoyed" his ill-gotten gains. The fact of dementia stealing Nathan's ability to think in those terms only partially registered with him.

His wife was a different matter. Vera had always looked well dressed and well-groomed whenever Joe saw her. Karen used to say that Vera bought quality clothing and toiletries and it showed. Joe remembered her tailored suits and pretty evening clothes. Whenever she came to Toronto she was ready for whatever events were happening. She was especially pleased when Joe and Karen had arranged for symphony tickets. Had Nathan spent his felonious money keeping Vera looking good?

Some things had been replaced around the living area but the bigger pieces of furniture were the same. Joe wondered if the sofa had been re-covered. He thought the micro-fibre must be a recent change.

Joe didn't know what he had expected from the house. Maybe a time-warp like the rooms upstairs. His memories were stuck with the 30-year-old furniture. He hadn't moved on but it seems his parents had to some extent.

Joe descended the ladder and stored the painting equipment under the porch.

Inside, television game-show contestants cheered their victories and groaned at their misses. Vera had a dictionary open in front of her. She referred to it whenever a word appeared that puzzled her.

Joe watched his mother with continued amazement at her seeming acceptance of her condition. He hadn't seen one moment of self-pity from her since he had arrived. Do you just plug along uncomplaining when the vital part of your life is in ruins? Find a way to cope and never complain. Is that the way she'd always been? Did she want to complain about Nathan's extra-curricular activities but didn't? Is she just quietly accepting of all that life hands her? He wondered what happened in their conjugal bed. No. he didn't want to think about that.

Joe's cell phone jarred him from his thoughts. He flipped it open and saw his ex-wife's name and number.

"Hello, Karen," he said. His tone was flattened with the possibility that this call would be trouble.

"Joe? I finally caught up with you. Doesn't anybody there answer their phone?" Karen was clearly feeling hassled and wanted Joe to feel her tension too.

"I'm busy here, Karen. Outside, painting."

"Well, I'm glad I finally got you. I've got a problem."

"What is it?" His words were almost spit from his mouth, the irritation of the last couple of hours spilling across the country to Toronto.

"You remember I have to travel to Texas this month? The head office wants all regional managers there."

"Yeah?" Joe said.

"Well, I can't leave Devon with Chantelle as I'd planned. Chantelle's sister has to have surgery. It's urgent. They think it's cancer. So she's flying to Halifax to be there for her. She'll be gone at least two weeks. Could be longer."

Karen let the implications sink in as the silence lengthened between them.

"So, you want me to find someone to keep Devon? Is that it?"

Karen waited a beat then said, "No, I want *you* to take him. You could have six whole weeks off if you take two weeks of vacation time. Why can't he go out there and be with you?"

Joe's reaction was swift and loud. "With me! Do you have any idea what I'm dealing with here? No, of course not!" he continued before Karen could answer, his churned-up emotions going into over-drive. "I'm trying to handle my mother who can't do anything for herself. And doing repairs on the house and...." He lost some momentum and took a deep breath.

"Well, surely there's help for her. She was alone before you arrived a few days ago." Karen's response was low-keyed logic. "And Devon can help with house repairs. He's 14-years-old, after all. He can paint, or whatever."

Joe started pacing the kitchen, letting Karen hang on the line. "I'm...somewhat overwhelmed here. She's so frail." His voice had lost its shrill edge as he walked out his tensions around the kitchen table.

"All the more reason for Devon to be there. He can help. You don't have to baby-sit him," Karen added.

"Have you talked to him about it?"

"Not yet. I wanted something arranged so he wouldn't feel he was being shunted around or a burden or something. Besides, you'd probably have to take some vacation days. I wanted to be sure that was happening before I told him."

Silence hung between them. "Joe? She said.

Joe sighed, giving in to the common sense of the situation. "Okay. Don't make the flight arrangements until I check that I can have vacation time. I'll call you later." He hung up. He scrubbed his hands through his hair, pressed his thumbs into his eyes. He could feel responsibilities piling up around him, crowding him. But if he could get vacation time bracketed with his usual hometime, he'd have almost six weeks off. At least he could spread the work out and not feel so pressured.

He grabbed a long-necked beer from the fridge and took deep pulls on it as he placed the call to the scheduler. When he was told he could have the requested time off he wasn't sure if that made life easier for him or if it would prove more difficult. His initial objections to Devon coming here surfaced again causing the cold beer to cramp in his stomach. These circumstances were less than ideal for a young teen. If Devon came here, this would be how he remembered his grandmother, shrivelled and struggling with basic needs. *He* hated to watch it happening. How would it affect a 14-year-old?

He sat back in his chair, sipped the beer and thought about how nice it would be to be flying a plane right about now.

☙

"You think I'm wallpaper, don't you?" Edie was leaning against the front door frame, arms crossed in an attitude of I'm-going-to-tell-you-a-thing-or-two.

Dono whirled around, obviously startled by the voice, as if confirming the statement. He relaxed again into a slouching stance, a cigarette smoldered between his fingers. He looked at Edie with a bored expression.

"Not a bad description, Edie. You never were on my radar." He dragged on the cigarette and half-turned away from her.

"You can ignore me but my life goes on. And everything that happened until now is still with me. What goes around comes around, Dono."

"What's that supposed to mean?"

"You figure it out."

"Are you threatening me?" Dono jerked his head upright and stared at Edie.

"Nobody lives a safe life. Haven't you learned that, Dono? She hesitated and considered her words. "Shit happens. It doesn't matter who you are."

"Yeah, well, I got my life under control. You should be so lucky."

"Are *you* threatening *me*, Dono?"

"Shit happens, Edie."

They each held their ground, staring the other down, Edie firmly against the door frame and Dono mastering the sidewalk.

In the back of the house Mel put the final items into Ty's duffle bag. She was taking as much time as she reasonably could, delaying the departure and Dono's possession of her son.

"I probably won't have any fun." Ty pouted. He was sitting on his bed, watching his mother pack his clothes for the weekend. His small, sad face nearly broke Mel's heart. The anger and frustration that gripped her made her want to throw things. It took everything in her to be calm in front of Ty.

"Oh, honey, I wouldn't say that. You always like going to cottages. That's what your dad said, that they were going to a cottage." Mel worked at keeping her voice neutral. Although she loathed Dono, she wouldn't frighten Ty by outbursts against his father. Later on he could think out things for himself, figure out what a selfish, egotistical, hostile, petty ... criminal his father was.

Dono hadn't always been hostile. When Mel first met him she thought he was polished and charming. She'd been attracted to her father's business associate, swept away by a degree of elegance rarely seen in a small town. When her eyes finally opened and his charm morphed into arrogance, she saw herself as Dono's ticket to a connection to her father. That connection alone was a strong reason for believing Owen and Dono were partners in crime. Dono's arrogance would lead him to think he could get away with anything. The fact that the police had scrutinized Dono's movements and questioned him extensively at the time of Owen's arrest confirmed for Mel that Dono was criminally involved. But the police found no probable cause to search his office and seize records.

Mel put T-shirts and shorts in Ty's duffel bag. She picked up Ty's purple dinosaur and wiggled it in the air. "Do you want to take Barney?" she asked.

Ty shook his head. "I'm not a baby." His tone was petulant and tears were close to the surface. "Can I come home if I want to?" he asked.

Mel felt a smile tug at the corners of her mouth and suppressed it. She sat beside Ty on the bed and pulled him to her. "Look, honey. Your dad doesn't see you very often and don't you think a cottage is one of the best places to visit him? One of the most fun places?" Ty was silent. "And if you have any problems you just call me and I'll work it out with your dad about coming to get you. Okay?"

Ty, still silent, bobbed his head. As Mel turned away to find his bathing suit, Ty put Barney into the duffel bag and tucked a T-shirt around him.

"So, I've put your inhaler into the bag. Tell me one more time when you'd use it." Mel had drilled this since Ty had started school and about the same time had started having nights with Dono.

"If I feel like I can't breathe or my chest and throat start to hurt and feel tight." He looked up at Mel with anxiety. "Does Dad know what to do?"

"Sure he does." Mel put on her brightest smile, wanting Ty to leave as reassured as possible. "He's seen us use it and I've talked to him a lot about it. No sweating it, okay?"

Ty nodded. Mel picked up the duffel, took Tyler's hand as they made their way to the door.

Mel squeezed past Edie who manned the doorway like a sentinel. Tyler held his mother's hand as long as possible. Dono was standing in hostile silence on the sidewalk and finally spoke when he saw Ty. "Hi, Sport. Let's go, eh. Got your swim suit?" Mel glared at the cigarette in Dono's hand. Dono threw it to the ground and stomped on it.

Ty raised his moist eyes to Mel. "See you, Mum." Dono clasped his son's hand and hustled him into the Lexus.

When they turned the corner out of sight Edie wilted. "I hate that man," she said. "I can't wait till Ty's old enough to refuse to go with him."

"Who's to say what will happen between now and then," Mel said. "Maybe we'll have a miracle and Dono will go to jail."

"And you'd keep Ty from visiting him ... just like you won't visit *your* father."

"He wouldn't deserve to be visited. Just like my father doesn't deserve it."

"But he's your father!"

Mel's voice was hard and tight. "And some role model he turned out to be. Nothing he did was an accident, Mum. He planned and executed fraud and took life savings from people."

"He made money for people. Nobody lost their life savings," Edie rationalized. "And if Owen deserves to be in prison you can bet Dono deserves it too," she said, as if accusing Mel's husband somehow diminished Owen's guilt.

"I just bet he does," Mel said vehemently. "And I hope one day it happens." She turned on her heel and left Edie to simmer on the porch.

"Well, I'm still going to visit Owen on Sunday!" Edie declared to Mel's retreating back.

· Chapter 4 ·

☙

Joe listened to Karen relay Devon's flight information. He'd have to drive into Vancouver by ten tomorrow morning.

"Why so fast? I didn't think you had to be in Houston 'till Wednesday."

"I've got non-stop meetings for three days. I don't know when I'll get home at night. This is the best thing to do."

"How is Devon taking this?" Joe popped a beer while he talked.

"Not too bad. Why don't you ask him?" Joe heard Karen passing the phone, then, Devon's man-child voice break. "Hi, Dad."

"Hey, Dev. Guess this is pretty unexpected, eh?"

"Guess so." Devon's flat tone spoke volumes.

"Well, we'll make it good. Okay?"

"I have to miss the Regional Skateboarding Championship." There was the edge of a whine in his voice.

"Are you in it?"

"No. I just want to go."

"Look, Dev. I'm sorry this is happening but your mom and I couldn't think of anything else. It was too sudden. We'll find some fun things to do. I've still got friends here. We'll do … stuff.

Maybe stuff you can't do in the city." Joe was improvising now. "Maybe something really west coast and you can dazzle your friends when you get home.

"Yeah, like what?" Devon was clearly skeptical.

Joe's mind was speed-dialing through possible teenage adventures. "Well ... maybe camping or rock climbing or kayaking. We'll find something. You think about it and I will too and then we'll talk tomorrow when you get here."

"Uh, is there a place to skateboard? Can I bring my skateboard?" It was an entreaty.

Joe knew conciliation when he heard it. "Sure, sure, bring it. I don't know areas for skating yet but I'll ask around. Okay? And bring your bathing suit."

"Sure, I guess. Here's Mom."

They rang off. He stretched and rolled his shoulders to ease the tension. That could have been worse.

Vera was at the kitchen table, finishing the dinner that Meals-On-Wheels had delivered in the afternoon. The Salisbury steak seemed to be a favourite, judging by the near empty plate and the amount of food debris around her mouth and over her clothing. Joe had watched her shuffle to find a small towel for her lap and then struggle with one hand before realizing he should help. Stunned by her neediness, he had cut the food for spearing with a fork, poured a glass of milk and had retreated to the phone.

He watched her now, swiping at her mouth with the towel, clearly intent on restoring order. Should he help her or let her do it herself? How was a person to know? She crumpled the towel onto the table and stood with her cane. Residual food scraps fell to the floor. She limped to the sink and ran water over her good hand and around her mouth, removing the remnants of the meal. She stood as erect as she could while she reclaimed her self.

Joe watched her and ached inside. She carried grace in her shriveled body. He felt stuck to his spot, impotent in the face of such dignity. He should be helping her in some way, but he couldn't move. He felt like weeping.

Vera smiled her soft smile as she made her way to the living room and Wheel of Fortune.

Then, Joe found that he couldn't do anything *but* move. He set the beer can hard on the counter and left through the front door just as Marika arrived to play crib.

∞

The voices coming from the living room were loud and angry. Ty pressed the covers around his ears. The room was dark except for a strip of light coming under the door to the hallway. A weak moon cast shadows through the narrow window. A tree branch splayed spider-like against the pane. He wanted to turn the light on but his father might see it under the door. He'd put him to bed and told him to go right to sleep.

He hadn't been sleepy. He laid on the cottage bunk-bed, confused about his father and his father's friend, Allison. She had kept smiling at him and asking if she could get him anything. Would he like a drink? Was he warm enough after his swim? How about a dry towel? Did he like Ketchup on his hamburger? Some times he'd answer her and some times he would just look at her, wondering if she really didn't know the answer to anything.

Most of the time Dono was on his cell phone. First he was yelling at some one, then, he was laughing. He rarely spoke to Ty. When Dono told him to go to bed Ty was glad. He'd read his Barney the Dinosaur book for a while then searched his backpack for his Spider-man figure. He pretended he was climbing a sky-scraper and saved a little boy from a fire. Then Spider-man rappelled down the building with the boy clinging to his neck. After a while he took Barney to bed with him. He'd settled under the covers clutching Barney and tried to close his eyes.

Now, Dono and Allison were in the living room yelling at each other, louder and louder. Allison's angry voice said he won't get away with it. Ty started to feel scared and he breathed more rapidly. Allison shouted, "I'll tell!" Something crashed and broke. He heard Allison's shrill cry.

Tyler wrapped the covers around his head to block out the sound. He rocked back and forth, tears running down his face. Now his breathing was noisy and he felt like he was choking.

He slid out of bed and felt for his backpack; he had to find his inhaler. The backpack straps tangled in the dark. He fumbled and couldn't grasp anything. T-shirts and toys were jumbled together. He frantically pulled clothes and toys from the bag and threw them across the floor.

By the time his fingers found the inhaler, his chest hurt so much he didn't think he could manage to make it work. He sucked in two puffs like he had been taught. He leaned against the bed, weak and sweaty with the effort of breathing. Ragged sounds squeezed through his swollen bronchi and his heart was racing. He was so scared he leaked into his pyjamas. He gasped and cried and rubbed his chest. He hoped the medicine would soon work and he'd be strong enough to find his father. His breathing eased fractionally but his chest was still too tight. He took two more puffs and crawled on his hands and knees to the doorway. He nudged the door open a crack and tried to call his father. As he lay by the door he breathed raspy whistles that died in the air.

In the living room, Allison shrieked that she hated Dono. Dono yelled that she could get out any time she wanted to. A door slammed and the cottage was silent.

❧

Joe circled the block. The Friday evening streets were crowded with people, hot and restless after a week of unrelenting heat. He wasn't sure where he was heading but it had to involve a beer. Traffic slowed in front of The Argyle, recently renamed The Red Fox Pub, a change that testified to the ambivalence of the owners' British leanings. Joe had known it as the local watering hole with a reputation for generously aging young patrons when he was 16-years-old and which had the added attraction of the only pool table in town. The Red Fox Pub would suit him fine.

A cold blast from the air conditioned room raised goose bumps as he waited for his pint of brew at the bar. He turned to a tap on the shoulder.

"Joey. Great to see you." Neil Heslop grinned at him. "Come sit with us. Elaine's just over there." He pointed out a table where several couples were pouring beer from pitchers dripping with condensation.

"Sure," he said. He followed Neil through the congested room, picking up an empty chair as he went.

"Hey, everybody," Neil said. "This is Joey. Used to live here eons ago. You can introduce yourselves." Names were murmured and handshakes all around. The women were pulling sweaters over their shoulders as the cooling effects of the beer and the air conditioning caught up with their shorts and T-shirts.

Joe looked around the room. Regardless of the name change, the interior was still lined with the darkly-wooded fibre-board that he remembered and held the faint scent of cigarette smoke from the decades before social responsibility eclipsed a night of indulging one's vices. Beside him, Neil was laughing, something about an apprentice at work making the most ignorant of mistakes.

"Hey, Joe," Neil said, "you ever have any close calls with the plane?" He leaned eagerly towards Joe.

"You really want to hear about problems with air planes?" Joe chuckled. "You'll never fly again," he smiled.

"Isn't everyone fascinated by near-misses?" Neil said. "All

those disaster shows on TV have a lot of viewers." He continued to look at Joe.

"Well, remember that plane that came into LAX with the twisted nose gear? CNN covered the landing, as only they can, with minute by minute analysis of how everything was going." Nods around the table. "I had something like that happen going into Comox air field once. Nose gear didn't come down. Had to shut down the engines. Lots of sparks and grinding metal. That was it."

That was enough to start talk about harrowing flight experiences and gave Joe opportunity to look around. He didn't recognize anyone. Thirty years adds weight and subtracts hair. In men anyway. The women looked so young, some of them. He could pick out the "lifers" with their age and vices written on their faces. Probably had their names tagged on the bar stools too.

His gaze kept returning to a woman with shoulder-length dark hair. It had the dense blackness of coffee too long on the stove. There was something about the way she held her head and the defiant lift to her chin. Her brows were heavy and her mouth outlined in red lipstick. She should have held a cigarette between the fingers she was waving at her companion.

When he could, Joe caught Neil's eye. "Who's that woman on the bar stool, next to the guy in the black muscle-shirt? She seems kind of familiar." He tipped his head towards the bar.

"Her? You should remember her. You had a hard-on for her all through high school," he grinned. "She was your neighbour. The one over the fence with the bikini and the big boobs." Neil nudged him in the ribs. "The Crossini girl, Elena. Now she's Elena Armstrong. That's her second husband's name, anyway. But they aren't together."

It was like a blow to the gut. Beer threatened to back up into his mouth. It hadn't occurred to him that he would run into her. Gone from the neighbourhood, gone for life. He averted his eyes and inhaled deeply. Joe didn't know if he could sit there and pretend Elena Crossini wasn't across the room. He reached for his beer to try for normality. He was relieved that his hand didn't visibly shake.

Neil was caught up in conversation across the table. Joe wanted to ignore the woman, pretend he didn't know she was there. But her presence was like a magnet drawing his eyes in her direction. Her companion punched her arm playfully and she threw back her head in a rolling laugh, her breasts straining against her white silk shirt. She reached up and stroked the side of his face, smiling like the cat with a bowl of cream. Now that he knew who she was, he couldn't mistake the arrogant toss of her head, the voluptuous way she used her body and relished the power she knew she had. She leaned back on the bar stool and crossed one tanned leg over the other with the relaxed confidence of a woman with her man wrapped up tight.

He had to leave. He swallowed the last of his beer and made his excuses. A drive to Vancouver tomorrow. Devon arriving. Yeah, it was unexpected.

The heat of the outdoors was less oppressive than the crushing atmosphere inside. He sat behind the wheel of the car and let the street sounds wash over him. He could get past this. At least she didn't live next door anymore.

ॐ

By 10 o'clock Mel had cooled enough to sit in the kitchen and open the *Real Estate Trading Services Licensing Manual*. This weekend without Tyler was precious solo time to tackle the first lesson. The house was still, Edie at a movie with their neighbour, Gert.

She perused the introductory chapter. Elements of the real estate market and land ownership and value, organization of the

Real Estate Brokerage Industry seeped into her consciousness but didn't hook to a memory cell. She scratched through her hair with both hands, vigorously stimulating alertness. This could be like slogging through wet sand. She needed to get into the spirit of the project and focus on her goal.

She got up to set the kettle to make an herb tea as the phone rang.

"Hello."

"Mel! It's Dono." Traffic noises threatened to drown out his voice.

"What do you want, Dono?" Mel got to the point.

Before Dono could finish Mel shrieked over his voice. "What happened to him? Where are you?" She gripped the phone like a lifeline. "Dono, where are you? Tell me what happened?"

"I found him …. He couldn't breathe. We're at the General. They've got him on oxygen and gave him some kind of medicine." His voice was a wrenching whisper.

"I'll be there in ten minutes." Mel dropped the phone into its cradle, whirled in the direction of the door, grabbed keys and her purse and slammed out of the house.

Mel ran into the ER and accosted the first person in uniform she saw. "Where's Tyler Harris?" Mel's terror etched her face with hard lines as her fingers squeezed the nurse's arm. The nurse released Mel's grip and took her hand. ""You're the mother? I'll take you to him."

Dono was sitting beside the gurney, head bowed. Ty's small body made a soft imprint under the sheet, his small face almost obscured by the oxygen mask. His eyes were closed, his breathing an audible rasp. An intravenous bag dripped saline into his arm.

Dono looked up. Mel's face told him he'd done enough and she would take over. He shifted the rolling stool and stood. "He's settled down a lot." Dono looked ready to bolt.

"What happened?" Mel's angry question brought Dono to a stop.

"I don't really know. He went to bed; he was fine. And when I found him he was on the floor by the bedroom door. I didn't hear anything."

"Who's the doctor here?" Her mouth was tight. She reached for Tyler's hand and gently stroked it.

"Avery... I think. I think that's what he said." Dono was edging to the door.

"Go have your cigarette." Mel didn't try to disguise her contempt. It was a dismissal.

Tyler's hand was soft and pliable. She cupped it between both of hers and moved it to her lips. She tried to hold back her tears. She swallowed with relief that his fingertips were warm and the colour good.

"So how's the young man doing?" A curly, red-head came around the drape. The man was wearing blue scrubs and a stethoscope was draped around his neck. Flecks of gray silvered his temples. "Hi. Are you the mother?"

Mel nodded. "Yes," she said softly. "Tell me what's happened so far."

"I'm Doctor Avery. I saw him when he came in. We gave him salbutamol — ventolin — by injection. To tell you the truth he was pretty far gone into respiratory distress. I was ready to do a trach and put him on a respirator if he didn't respond quickly. Fortunately he started to come around. It was a close one. There's a ventolin in the nebulizer mixed with oxygen. We're keeping the I.V. open just as a precaution. He seems to be settling."

Mel blinked back tears. "Thank you," she said.

"I want to admit him for tonight, at least. He needs more treatment and monitoring. He's exhausted but could be okay to go home tomorrow."

Gwen Enquist

Mel nodded, couldn't think of questions to ask. "Who's the doctor who cares for his asthma?" Dr Avery asked. "I'll talk to him and fill him in on this episode."

Mel nodded again and gave the details the doctor wanted, found Tyler's medical care card then sat beside her sleeping son. She swallowed silent tears and watched Tyler's pale face and his small chest breath in and out until they transferred him to a hospital room.

· Chapter 5 ·

☙

Traffic on Trans-Canada Highway 1 east was heavy and slowed to a crawl at exit points for popular tourist spots. Joe sighed in resignation. The car's air conditioning system was maxed out and gave off clicking noises in protest. The air was still heavy. Devon was plugged into his iPod nano, a Christmas gift from Joe. He air-guitared the rhythms from some digital space and gave little notice to the landscape, the heat, or his father.

When Joe had picked his son up at Vancouver International Airport an hour previously, he had looked at Devon fondly and suddenly realized that life had just gotten more complicated. Over the last few months Devon had morphed into a skateboarder with board-shorts that hung low and loose and spiked bleached hair that glowed around his head. Up close, adolescent acne dotted his forehead and a brow piercing drew attention to this inflamed zone. He leaned into his father for a hug while clutching his skate board to his chest with one hand and, with the other, hitching his shorts into the safety zone.

Now Joe had to bring this 21st century kid, this boarding-dude, into the stultifying quietness of an invalid's home. He had forgotten the brash impact that the teen-aged Devon made. He had forgotten because he didn't live with him. Until now he could send him home after a weekend and relish his peace. This time it was different.

They had to talk. He had to get Devon to understand the situation at his grandmother's house. Her frailty, her diminished life, her needs. There had been nothing but silence from the passenger seat, just the air-guitar that had filled the space for miles now. Should he insist that Devon unplug himself and talk? Or should he just take-it-as-it-comes, deal with issues as they arise?

Joe took exit #119, Vedder Road, to the city centre. The change of pace and direction caught Devon's attention. He looked around and said, "Are we close to Grandma's house?"

"Yeah. About five minutes." With some hesitation Joe continued. "Dev, we haven't had a chance to talk about Grandma." He paused. "You know she's had a stroke, don't you? That it's affected how she gets around and manages at home."

"Yeah, Mom told me. You came to help her sell the house. And I'm supposed to help too."

"That's right. But more than that you have to understand that she's not like you remember. Not lively or fun or talkative. Do you know what a stroke does?"

"Sort of. Mom said it affects parts of your brain so you can't work your body as well."

"Yeah. That's right. But it causes more problems than most people think about. You know, we do things everyday that we take for granted, like brushing our teeth or feeding ourselves, going to the bathroom? That sort of thing. Sometimes a stroke makes that hard or impossible. Grandma's having some difficulties and needs help. For one thing, she uses a cane and drags her foot. Sometimes she drools. I want you to understand these things before we get there."

"Sure ... I get it. She's different. It'll be cool. Don't worry." He plugged the ear buds in again.

"And, Devon," he touched his son's arm to ensure his attention, "she needs a quiet house, a quiet routine."

"Sure. Sure. I get it. No sweat." Devon returned to the silent music.

Joe pulled into the driveway and parked in front of the garage. Devon bounded out of the car, slamming the door and shouting for his grandmother. Joe followed and promised himself patience.

The television flickered from the hallway. Vera was settled on the couch with a card table in front of her, crossword puzzles on the go. Joe stopped in the hallway while Devon steamrolled into the living room.

"Grandma! Hi!" Devon said. He slouched down beside her and hugged her tightly. Vera's eyes teared and she mouthed Devon. She reached and flipped off his cap and stroked his bleached hair with her good arm. Her eyes sparkled while a line of saliva tracked down her chin. Devon grabbed a tissue and patted her mouth. "Hi, Gram," he said softly.

~

Mel dragged her weary body through the hospital lobby. At 9 a.m. the hospital was buzzing with activity. She needed sleep. It had been a long night beside Tyler's bed, watching every breath, breathing in tandem with him as if it would boost his oxygen level.

She had just left Tyler's bedside for a shower and nap when Edie had come to replace her. Edie had slept at home after a midnight visit to see Tyler and to cry and hold Mel tight.

With the morning light Tyler was awake and restless about his confinement. His doctor had been pleased with Tyler's progress but told them it had been a close call. The intravenous could come out but he wanted Tyler to spend another day and night to rest and to monitor the medication routine.

Mel moved along the hospital entrance corridor, so overcome with tiredness that she collided with a woman coming the other way through the door. She started to apologize, then, recognized Allison, Dono's secretary and girlfriend. Each looked at the other with a furtive glance and started to move on. Then Mel swung around.

"Hey! I want to know what happened at the lake last night. Tyler could have died. Tell me. What went on?" She stared at Allison, unwavering and determined.

"It's none of your business … that's between Dono and me." She stopped, turned away, then, turned back. "What do you mean, Tyler? He went to bed. That's all."

"That's not all." Mel's jaw was clamped tight. "Tyler nearly died there last night and you say it's none of my business?"

"Well, he was fine when I … left." Allison raised her head defiantly. "I didn't stay after about ten."

With Allison's chin at that angle Mel could see the blue-purple colouration of a bruise over her cheek bone. "Dono got physical, didn't he? I can see it on your face." Allison shrank backwards. "And I can only guess that a visit to the hospital today means there's more to it than that." Mel took a threatening step forward. "Tell me what you know … or, I swear …."

"I don't know anything! I was gone by ten o'clock. Dono … and I had an argument. Tyler was in bed." Tears flowed down Allison's face. "Is Tyler okay?"

"Now. No thanks to either of you. He had a bad asthma attack. Dono says he found him on the floor by the bedroom door." Mel's voice was whispery and moist.

"Oh," Allison whispered. She turned away. "I'll be late … x-ray."

Mel's head came up. "X-ray? Did he break something?"

Allison shrugged. "Maybe. Maybe my rib." She lowered her eyes and turned away, then back again. "I'm finished with him," she said. "I hope Tyler's okay." She hurried down the hallway.

Mel watched Allison's retreating back. The fact that Dono was capable of violence didn't surprise her. She had seen his volatile temper, had experienced rough handling when he didn't get his way. When he was high he was a stick of dynamite simmering under the surface of a charming swagger. She also knew that something major had contributed to Tyler's attack. When she'd had some rest and Tyler could talk to her, she had a few questions that needed answers.

☙

Joe didn't know if lunch had been a disaster or a triumph. It had started with Vera pointing out to Devon that she had a sandwich waiting for her in the fridge. Devon then started teasing that some sandwich fairy had been here and why wasn't that something he'd been told as a kid? How'd he missed that? Vera shook her head in denial, a grin tugging her right cheek upward. Devon insisted that it wasn't fair and did the fairy leave a menu? Could Gram choose her own sandwich? And if she could, could she please ask for ham and cheese next time? They'd race to the fridge and whoever got there first won the sandwich. Oh sure, he'd give her a break. Let her go first off the starting block. After all, she had to manoeuvre the cane, but besides that everything was equal, so ….

Devon and Joe sat at the table across from Vera. Joe was stunned at the way Devon acted with his grandmother, just like everything was … normal. Joe couldn't quite grasp what was happening. Devon's teasing didn't stop throughout the meal. Vera grinned around her chewing and sandwich filling rolled down her chin. Devon noticed when she needed a napkin and passed her one, indicating she should wipe her mouth. Once she choked and sputtered and Devon was quick to settle her and offer water. She was grinning when he sat again. When her glass of milk shifted dangerously close to the table edge, Devon moved it to safety without breaking the momentum of his inane banter.

At the end of the meal, food debris covered the table. There was egg salad over Vera's eye where she had waved her hand to try to keep up with Devon's kidding. Her hands were slimed with mayonnaise. Devon said he'd help her wash but she waved him away. She limped her way to the sink and rinsed away the evidence of the meal. She turned from the sink and looked at Devon, smiling with absolute delight. Devon smiled back.

Joe guessed the meal had been a triumph. An afternoon of work wouldn't be nearly as much fun.

"Mom, would you like Devon to stay here with you while I work outside?"

Vera shook her head. "I need rest." She grinned. "Too much fun." She turned loving eyes towards Devon. "Make him wear off energy." Each word was enunciated. She thumped away to the living room.

Joe knuckled Devon playfully on the arm, pleased with how things were going. "I'm going to put on some old clothes. I'll show you the room you'll use." Joe edged into the hall. "I think I've scraped most of the house. I'll show you how things are going then we can decide if we should work today or not."

Devon bounded up the stairs, two at a time. Joe eyed him with envy.

Once outside, with the sun beating down from a clear blue sky, Joe sent Devon back for the protection of a T-shirt and cap. They eyed the building and decided they could finish a certain section then call it a day.

"We won't work too long, Dev. It's too hot." Devon nodded, ear buds already plugging his ears. Joe climbed a ladder and started on some window trim. Devon took the easier place on the porch and began painting the porch railings. The iPod nano was clipped to the waist of his baggy shorts. He bounced to music only he could hear. Most of the paint found its target and the remainder splattered Devon's bare legs.

Joe smiled and marveled at Devon's buoyant nature that carried him with apparent ease through a splattered, mucked-up lunch to working in the hot sun, and enjoying it.

As Joe concentrated on the edges of the window trim, movement in the yard next door caught the corner of his vision. An elderly woman tottered down the steps, picked up a watering can and filled it from the tap. Joe stopped painting mid-stroke as he recognized Mrs. Crossini. She was stoop-shouldered and walked with the stiffness of age in her knees. Her lined face betrayed the 30 years since Joe had last seen her. Her hair had greyed but had retained a youthful fullness and framed her round face.

He hadn't thought about her still living there. After seeing Elena last night and hearing about her marriages he had just assumed that time had scattered the rest of the family. His mother never mentioned her. But she wasn't likely to. As far as Joe knew, Vera and Mrs. Crossini had avoided each other from the time Elena had matured into the subject of town gossip.

Joe realized he was staring and pulled back to his work, but couldn't pull his mind into line. How old had Elena been when rumours had linked her name with Nathan's? Maybe, sixteen. No older. Joe had known about it since he was about twelve. The furtive meetings in the garage hadn't escaped Joe's notice, or his mother's. That took some guts. And an incredible lust and willingness to demean himself.

Neil was way out in left field when he said that Joe had had a case for Elena. His father's affair had been flaunted right under their noses. Joe couldn't help but notice Elena. Everyone noticed Elena.

Mrs. Crossini watered her flowers and went back indoors. The uneasy feeling he'd had in this yard a few days ago had returned. Whenever Nathan had entered the house through the back door he'd carried his damaged spirit with him. Joe could remember tension hanging in the atmosphere, anger erupting at unpredictable times and places. He felt his father's shame and his mother's humiliation. And yet, Vera had done nothing. Eventually, the town was talking. Eventually, Joe did something about it and left town soon after.

What a difference between this house and the sense of contentment he'd felt at Scott's cottage, sitting in the still night, watching distant stars. Before they separated and were struggling with their relationship, Karen had called him cynical, said he had never learned to trust or love deeply. Can a place empty out a person? Leave him without the necessary substance to build relationships? Did it all start here? And end with his marriage in shambles? Realistically, he knew that a place couldn't send out corrupting vibrations that clung like fog wrapped around you. But he found it hard to see the world through any other lens.

He studied Devon, so happy and upbeat, painting and keeping time to his music and contrasted that with his own angry childhood. Suddenly he was overcome with a primal feeling that Devon needed protection, needed to be sheltered from danger so he wouldn't end up soul-battered for life. The feeling was brief but intense. He recognized Devon's sunny personality and admired it in his son; it could only come from love and security in his life. That had a lot to do with Karen; he had to give her that. Joe saw no signs of the self-absorbed, know-it-all, assertiveness of many teens, nor the infuriating petulance that drove parents to give up their role as responsible decision-makers.

He had never brought Devon to visit his grandparents in their home. Now, putting Devon into this yard triggered this deep instinct to protect. Things seemed good now, but he was only fourteen. There were destructive influences out there in the world that would touch Devon some day. Joe still had time to strengthen the sense of security and belonging his son seemed to have.

"Heh, Dev!" he called. Devon jerked around. His father had managed to break into the digital zone.

"Let's call it a day. It's too hot," he said.

"All right," he said enthusiastically. "I'm with you," Devon smiled.

"Listen. I've got a friend with a cottage on a lake. What do you say to a swim?"

"I say, let's go," he grinned.

They found Vera napping on the sofa, soft snores punctuating the quiet. Joe muted the television and wrote a note telling Vera they were gone for a few hours.

Scott's cottage on Heron Bay Road was a 30 minute drive from Sycamore Street. When it came into view Joe took a deep breath and exhaled. He felt his shoulder muscles loosen. The aging wood structure had changed little in thirty years, except that it seemed smaller. The cedar shake siding, the pitched roof with curled-edged shingles, the cedar decking aged to silver, all invoked memories of wiener roasts, swimming in the early spring chill and nights by lamp-light playing Monopoly.

When he'd been here the other night he had felt the tentacles of memory wrap around him and squeeze him softly. Today, with the sun beating down and Devon beside him, he could almost hear the splash of a diver coming off the raft and the calls to friends, 'It's time. It's been an hour. Last in is a rotten egg!' Using logs as floats and sinking them, underwater breath-holding contests, the memory of someone's mother sitting sentry on the shore. It all felt so special, so right.

He looked at Devon as they walked the slope down to the cottage. Devon's eyes were bright, taking in the cottage and expanse of clear blue lake out front. This was Devon's kind of place, he decided. Both Devon and the lake held a charm and innocence unusual to the 21st century. He found himself wanting Devon to love it.

Scott and Marion were sitting at the water's edge. Scott dangled his feet off the dock into the lake. The faint glow of a sun burn spotted his shoulders. Marion sat in a low beach chair that was anchored by her weight to the shoreline, her legs fully immersed in the lake. A large flat sun hat shadowed her face. Two young boys tossed a foam football, forcing the receiver into a long swim to return the throw. "Good throw, Jeremy," Marion called.

"Hope we're not interrupting," Joe said.

Marion and Scott turned in unison and smiles spread across their faces.

"Hey, Joe! Great that you came down," Scott called. He got to standing on the dock. "Hey! Who's this young guy with you?"

"Scott, Marion, I'd like you to meet Devon, my son," Joe said. Scott and Marion came towards Joe and stretched out a welcoming hand to greet Devon.

"Great time for you to come, Joe. No other visitors and our boys just got back from their grandparents' place. Hey, Jeremy, Richie, come and meet our friends."

With introductions done, Jeremy and Richie took Devon into the cottage to change into his bathing suit. Joe sat on the dock beside Scott and touched his feet to the water. It was colder than he remembered.

Joe told Scott and Marion about Devon's unexpected arrival and the fact of his prolonged stay in Chilliwack. Well, if the weather remained this hot, they all agreed that it was better than a summer in Toronto.

"Come out and swim whenever you want. It'll be good for both of you," Marion said.

"You know what? Devon brought his skateboard with him. I hope he sees the lake as a much better choice," Joe said.

"The lake will grow on him fast. Why don't you stay for supper?" Marion put up her hand to stop Joe's polite protest. "Tonight is bison burgers on the barbeque. No big deal. And I made a chocolate cake for dessert. Maybe that will help you make up your mind," she teased.

Joe thanked her, recognizing what a great break this was, not to be returning to a night in a hot house with a young teen and watching Jeopardy! for fun. Vera would be okay. As she pointedly said, she got along on her own before he came.

Marion stayed at the water's edge with the boys while Scott and Joe made their way to the deck and a cold beer. They settled on the shady side of the porch and tipped their beers in salute to each other.

"You know," Scott said, "a summer out here with the lake and bush so close will probably do you good." Joe looked at him, not quite catching his meaning.

"I mean, who wants to work in the summer? Even if it is flying planes. And Toronto has to be next to hell in July and August," Scott added.

Joe considered the hellish temperatures and humidity he had left behind. He lifted his beer to Scott and with a sweep of his arm that included the lake he said, "This does have compensations, doesn't it?"

"Joey, I even take Sundays off in the summer. Lots of realtors don't. Things slow somewhat and pick up again in the fall. But life's too short and so are summers at the lake. You know, in five years Jeremy will be eighteen. That will pass in a flash. Then two years later Richie could be gone too. Who knows where they'll end up. Marion and I decided that I could pass up some commissions in favour of family time here."

Joe sat there, thinking over what Scott was saying. This was a rare opportunity to spend time with Devon. And seeing how well Devon and his grandmother began, maybe it wouldn't be so bad having Devon around as a help and buffer. That was the truth of it. It wasn't only the house that was a problem to him. He had trouble being around his mother. Her infirmities, and the way an everyday event, like eating, had degenerated to the point of ... of being disgusting. Shove the food in, never mind the mess, get the sustenance you need, be done with it. He could hardly believe he was thinking this way. He needed Devon right now as much as Devon needed him.

"I have nearly six weeks with Devon. I guess I can think of ways to make the most of it," Joe said.

Scott smiled at him then turned to yell something at the kids. By now Devon was in on the water football. Joe watched Devon stretch for the throw. With his hair plastered down Joe saw his own bone structure appear. Devon looked so much like him. He felt a tug to be that kid again. The one that was carefree and laughing, playing in the lake. He had to tell himself again that's it is people that matter, not places. But, damn, this cottage and lake had a hold on him. But so did the family house. The feelings they evoked were opposites. One made him happy and lightened his spirit. The other oppressed and agitated him.

The boys came scrambling up the bank, ran past the cottage to the bush behind. "We're going to show Devon what we found in the back," Jeremy called over his shoulder.

"What'd they find in the back?" Joe asked.

"They found a burrow that seems to be a rabbit hole. Richie says he saw a rabbit go down and Jeremy thinks there are babies there."

"This place is wonderfully different than Toronto. Life is simpler here. Kids never get that natural experience in the city," Joe said.

"We're lucky in a way," Scott said. "For us this place is a choice. Not everybody gets to choose."

"No, not all parents get to choose, or maybe they just choose wrong." Joe's voice was low and pensive. Scott looked at him. "I went and saw my father. Mom has a routine of going to see him on Thursdays now instead of every day. I took her there. I've been twice now." He looked up at Scott. "He doesn't know me. Thinks I'm his brother, Will."

"Christ," Scott murmured.

"He made some bad choices in his life, made me pretty angry. But even I wouldn't choose this for him."

"How's it affecting your mother?"

"It's strange. She seems to take it in her stride. He doesn't know her either. Thinks she's Mary, Mom's mother. She doesn't cry or seem anguished. She just goes in and sits with him, gives him some juice. Takes him gummie bears every week. It's actually creepy the way he looks so blank and she sits there looking after him, patting his chin dry. Like, this-is-what-life-has-handed-me-so-get-on-with-it." Joe looked up at Scott. "Are we made of stuff that strong? Or did that die out with their generation?"

"Oh, some of that strength has trickled down the line. You just have to look at Mel to see it. Her situation is pretty tough. But she's determined on a certain path for herself as a single parent. She's made her own choices that don't involve getting any help from Tyler's father."

"That's a hard line to take. I hope it works for her," Joe said.

"Choices are just that — choices. Some work and some don't."

"Is it generational, the choice to stay in a marriage? I mean, I've wondered why my mother didn't leave Nathan early on. Everybody knew she was getting a raw deal. But she stayed. It was like she put blinders on and didn't see the fallout happening."

"Maybe it's generational. What were her prospects as a single parent?" Scott said. "She didn't have any skills. And women stayed in bad marriages more then."

"She's so stoic. Guess she's been there before," Joe said. "Christ! If I had a stroke and had to contend with what she does — I don't think I could do it." Joe sighed.

Marion climbed the steps of the deck. The sombre atmosphere dissipated as Marion began chatting and making supper preparations. Scott lit the barbeque and eventually they called the boys from their back-yard adventure.

Devon enthused about the rabbit hole. He thought he saw movement down there. It was, "way cool."

After eating, with the boys claiming the kitchen table to play Rummoli, the three adults relaxed with Remy Martin served in plastic glasses. "So civilized," Joe quipped as they raised their glasses. They watched the play of the late sun on the water in the bay. Streaks of orange, bleeding into pink, cast a warm July glow. Joe left the real world behind as he sat here.

The phone rang and the real world intruded on everyone. Marion rose to find her cell phone and screen whatever call seemed necessary. The men heard her speaking. When she put her head out the door for Scott, there were worry lines on her brow.

"I think you'll want to talk to Mel. Tyler's in the hospital. He's okay now. But she wants to talk to you."

Scott took the phone and spoke quietly with Mel while Marion and Joe waited on the deck. When Scott came back he said, "Thank God he's all right. It sounded like a close call." He looked at Marion. "We'll check tomorrow but she said he's getting out of hospital in the morning." He turned to Joe. "Tyler had a bad asthma attack. He was with Dono for the weekend. Mel's really upset. Thinks Dono caused this."

"It wouldn't surprise me," Marion said. "Poor Mel." Then more thoughtfully, "Poor Tyler."

Poor Mel, indeed, Joe thought. Dealing with a bastard of a husband and a sick kid. Again, a number of choices to get to that point, but ....

Joe glanced into the cottage. Devon had his hand of cards in one hand while he cradled his head in his other arm stretched out on the table.

"Looks to me like the time difference finally caught up with Devon. I'd better take him home."

He gathered Devon who didn't object to the idea of bed. As they left, Marion invited them for dinner the next night. Joe hesitated at the excess of hospitality but agreed when she said they always liked company on the weekends and that he could bring a salad and drinks.

On the way home when he asked Devon what he thought of the cottage on the lake, Joe thought he heard way cool from his sleepy son and was glad

· Chapter 6 ·

Mel pressed the off-button on the phone. She relaxed for the first time in three days. Tyler could come home. When both Mel and Edie heard the whine in his voice about being in hospital, Mel knew that he was well. She offered a silent thank you to whatever deities hovered over her house right now.

Meanwhile, Edie was preparing to go to see her husband, Owen, in the medium security institution in Abbotsford, a short hour away by bus. Mel's anger at her mother's misguided devotion to Owen simmered. Mel hated this Sunday routine. She spent every Sunday in an agitated state while Edie gathered magazines and Owen's treat of the week, two Oh Henry! bars. She slammed cupboard doors and splashed cleaner too forcefully around the kitchen sink and counter-tops. Her tension always surfaced as a cleaning frenzy until Edie was gone and Mel could will herself to think about other things. Today she would think about Tyler and what he recalled of the night he had the asthma attack. One thing she was certain about, and that was that she would never allow Tyler to spend nights with Dono again.

"We need to go soon." Edie was standing in the hallway, tote bag over her arm. "The bus goes at 10:10."

Mel clamped her teeth together. "I know when the bus goes," she said. She opened the fridge to consider what needed stocking and to delay the inevitable collaboration with her mother's Sunday duty.

Edie saw her visits to the prison as a duty. Owen's conviction had thrown Edie into financial disaster, but she supported Owen because he was her husband. He was family. She and Mel argued every Sunday about what duty is owed to a family member who is a criminal. Edie stood her ground with you-don't-kick-a-person-when-he's-down.

"Mel," Edie said. "Stop banging things around. It's time to go."

Mel banged the fridge door. She grabbed her purse, walked around Edie and out the door.

Edie called to Mel's back, "You're so full up with anger that there's no room for grief. This is a situation for grieving," she yelled. "You just keep shoving the grief aside and pressing it away. Well, it won't go away. It'll just wait till the anger loses its edge." Now she was talking to Mel through the windshield, more quietly. "In a quieter time the grief will slip back in and you'll surprise yourself with tears." She sat in the passenger seat and regarded her daughter's tight face. "One day that anger will leak away and grief will pour in," she finished.

Mel had heard it before. She could make out her mother's sniffling as they drove along, but Mel refused to let go of her anger and be drawn in by Edie's tears. When Mel stopped to let Edie out of the car she saw Allison enter the station. She couldn't miss this chance. She had Tyler's story, as much as he could remember. She had to pin down more facts about Dono's recent behaviour. She followed Edie into the station.

When Allison turned from the ticketing booth, Mel stepped into her path. "We need to talk some more," she said. "Let's go outside." Allison's mouth dropped open.

"Where are you going," Mel asked.

83

"It's really none of your business," Allison said.

"Well, it is when it involves my son and his father. Tyler told me he heard lots of loud arguing and he got scared. That's what started his asthma attack. You did have something to do with the argument, didn't you?" Mel accused.

Allison took a step back. "I didn't have anything to do with Tyler being sick. As far as I knew he was fine." She broke eye contact with Mel and asked, "How is Tyler now?"

"I'm picking him up at the hospital as soon as I leave here." Mel softened her voice, hoping Allison wouldn't turn away. "He's okay, now. If you had nothing to do with Tyler's bad experience, then I guess it's all Dono's fault. I'm not surprised."

"Probably," Allison said.

"Dono has a lot of suppressed rage. He lets loose some times, especially if he's been using." Mel's voice was low and neutral, not attaching any collateral blame to Allison. She was clearly letting Allison off the hook.

"I have a broken rib," Alison offered.

"Yeah, I figured," Mel said. She knew that if Allison was going to say more she couldn't come on as threatening. She had to make her feel safe, that Mel was an ally who understood and sympathized. She put a victims-in-this-together quality to her voice

"I left him because I could see where things were heading," Mel said. "One night he twisted my arm back so far I thought he might break it." She looked at Allison, hoping she would offer something too. "It happened so quickly. His moods are unpredictable. He was all sweetness and then suddenly he was in a rage. We were talking about my father and his guilt or innocence in the fraud charges. He couldn't handle talking about the case. He couldn't handle a lot without drugs to prop him."

"Me too," Allison said softly.

The bus roared to life beside them drowning out Allison's words.

"Pardon?" Mel said.

"He got mad at me too, suddenly, about the case. I didn't want to deal with the fallout anymore. I told him that."

"What fallout?"

Allison couldn't hold Mel's eyes. She looked around and moved towards the bus. "Just stuff in the office. Accounts and stuff." She was at the bus door. "I have to go."

"What accounts? Where are you going? Maybe we should talk again."

Allison shook her head and was lost to the long interior of the bus.

Edie came out of the station, her ticket in her hand. Mel pulled her aside. "Keep your eyes on Allison. See where she gets off."

"Why? Where do you think she's going?"

"I don't know, but she's running away from Dono."

Edie nodded. "I'll be back on the afternoon bus."

Just minutes later Mel arrived at the hospital parking lot. Tyler was waiting in his room with his few belongings in a plastic bag.

"I thought you'd never come," he said. "I've been waiting and waiting." He was still pale from his ordeal.

"Hi, Sweetie. I had to take Grandma to the bus. You know. It's Sunday."

"When can I go to see Grandpa? You said when I'm bigger, if I still want to. I'm bigger now."

"Not big enough, Sport," she bit her lip. She hated it when she used Dono's nick name.

Soon in the parking lot, Mel buckled Tyler into his seat. Dono's silver Lexus pulled up beside her.

"I thought I could see Tyler again before he went home," Dono said. "Hi, Ty. You feeling better?" Dono tried to move around Mel to get close to Tyler.

"This is how you'll be seeing him from now on, Dono. With me beside him," Mel said.

"What are you on about? I didn't do anything, Mel. I got him to hospital when he needed to go. You can't say I didn't."

Mel wasn't impressed with Dono's defense. She glared at him. She grabbed Dono's upper arm and moved them both several car-spaces away so that Tyler wouldn't hear. Mel, firm and angry, leaned in to Dono's face.

"I know you were fighting with Allison. And I know it scared Tyler into that terrible asthma attack. If you think you can deny you're part of the problem, you're mistaken." Her face hardened and she pulled up straight. She clenched her jaw and poked Dono's chest with her finger. "I'm not afraid of you Dono. Not now. I'll fight you for Tyler with everything in me. From now on you only get to see him in circumstances that I approve."

Dono exploded. "What? You can't do that! I have visitation rights!"

"And if you try to exercise them except when I say you can, I'll take you back to court and make sure that you don't see him at all!"

They stood three feet apart, tense, eager for the other to make the first move. Mel broke the stalemate.

"It's my way or nothing, Dono. Do you really want to take this to court?"

"I'll see him. I swear I'll see him." Dono strode back to Tyler's side and spoke to him through the opened window. Then he turned quickly and, with fury pushing him, accelerated the car out of the parking lot.

ã

For Joe, Sunday morning had a routine — he was either flying or sleeping. Today he slept. Devon hadn't surfaced either. By the time Joe was sufficiently awake to go to the kitchen, it was nearly eleven o'clock.

Devon was stirring too, calling for a towel and face cloth, and wondering why the room he slept in was so girly. He still looked sleepy when he reached the kitchen.

"That was your Aunt Sandra's room," Joe explained.

"Yeah? Where is she?" Devon asked.

"She lives in Australia. She went down there after college and stayed."

"Wow, that's cool." Devon poured milk while Joe made toast. "Will I get to meet her some day?"

"Well, who knows? Australia's easier to get to than it used to be." Joe eyed his son. A trip to Australia. Could happen.

"Where's Gram?"

"I think in the bathroom." He paused. "Say, is there anything you want different for breakfast? Like cereal or an egg? I'm not totally helpless. I just don't know what's in the house."

"Nah, this is fine."

"We can go shopping later. I have to pick up salad stuff and drinks to take to the lake."

They painted for two hours. The sun was unrelenting. Both Joe and Devon had head scarves covering their hair and necks. Joe took another gulp of water from the bottle on the porch. "Dev? I think we could suffer if we stay out here any longer."

He didn't have to say it twice. Devon was indoors in seconds.

"Dev, drink some more water and put a cool cloth on your head and neck." Joe found clean tea towels and each wiped himself down.

"We'll rest a bit then go out."

"How does Gram manage in the heat?" Devon asked.

"Actually, she seems pretty good. She wears loose dresses and doesn't move around much."

"Can she come shopping with us?"

"Well, I…."

"We could stop for an ice cream. She can handle that in one hand." Devon's face was eager.

"Well … I guess it could work. Go ask her." This wasn't on Joe's agenda. Maybe she'd say no.

"Hey! Gram thinks it's a cool idea."

Joe could tell by the state of the kitchen that Vera had had her lunch. There were fuzzy milk stains on the table and a bread crust had rolled under the chair. He wondered how much lunch was on Vera's clothes.

Joe decided that a fast-food restaurant with a picnic table was the best choice. Vera could sit to eat her ice cream while he and Devon got some lunch and then went shopping. He grabbed a box of tissues on the way out.

Devon guided his grandmother to a picnic bench. "I'll get your ice cream, Gram. What flavour?"

"Vanilla," she said.

"Gram," he said seriously, "are you kidding? There's a whole art to picking ice cream. Vanilla's a wuss flavour. They give that to people who are sick. That's for when you have the flu. No, you need a flavour with presence that says something about you, something with a touch of class. What about strawberry? That's the kind they serve in fancy little dishes with silver spoons. That's the one for you," he declared.

Vera was grinning and nodding.

"Now, me — I need something that's going out on a limb. Something on the wild side. Nothing like rocky road. Everybody gets rocky road. That's like the latte of ice cream. And not bubble-gum. It hits you in the face with colour and flavour, but, let's face it, it's for kids."

By this time Vera was laughing so hard she was sputtering to control the drool on her chin.

Devon was unstoppable. "Now, me, I need a manly flavour, one that takes strength and confidence to order. What do you think of tiger paws? Licorice and orange. Yeah, that's manly."

Vera grinned. "Strawberry has class," she said.

Joe just shook his head in wonder and went inside to order.

Minutes later Joe was back with pizza and an ice cream cone. "Dev, see that Safeway down the block?" Devon nodded. "Why don't you stay here with Grandma and I'll go shop there. I won't be more than fifteen minutes."

Devon was working on a pizza slice and nodded agreement. Joe gave him money to buy his own ice cream. Vera licked at a dripping strawberry cone and Devon passed tissues to her.

Joe bought double the amounts he thought he needed for everything. Next door was a liquour store where he bought beer and wine. When he got back to Devon and Vera, Devon was demonstrating the best skateboarding stance. His knees were slightly bent and arms extended for balance. He was explaining the dynamics to Vera and she nodded and smiled like she understood and cared. Then Devon executed a tight 180 degree jump, turned and landed in front of her, arms extended, with a grand, "Ta da! See, Gram."

Vera was smiling. Pink ice cream was now part of the mosaic of food stains on Vera's clothes. Joe found it didn't bother him as much as it did a few days ago. Vera's frailty was less visible as she sat on a bench in the sun. The air around her carried the scent of summer. The light and freshness imbued her with a naive vitality, much like Devon's.

The Vera who sat in the sun was such a contrast to the one in the old house. In the house, an air of neglect and end of life stagnation seemed to cling to her. Whenever Joe looked at her, he saw that pitiful image.

As Joe watched, a hummingbird darted to Devon's ice cream and hovered there. Vera gasped with an opened-eyed smile and uttered, "Oh, oh." She was clearly enthralled. The bird flew away. This was a different person than the one that inhabited Joe's mind. This woman had the ability to feel delight, and to marvel at the beauty around her.

Joe watched Vera clean drool from her chin. He struggled with the two versions of his mother. He still had trouble knowing how to treat her but he figured the outing hadn't done any harm.

※

Tyler was napping on the couch when the phone rang. He stirred but didn't waken as Mel answered the phone.

"Hi, Scott. Thanks for phoning."

"We want to know about Tyler, of course."

"He's home. Napping right now. He's tired but, other than that, seems back to normal."

"That's great. So good to hear. Do you think he could handle coming out here for lasagna? Marion made a big pan. Nothing that would over-exert him."

Mel thought for a minute. "Okay. If he doesn't run around today he should be fine. But I have to pick my mother up at the bus at five o'clock."

"That's fine. Bring Edie too. You'll be out here before we're ready to eat."

"Okay. Tell Marion I'll bring a fruit salad." Then, before she rang off, "Scott, I want to talk to you about Dono too. Maybe we can have a few minutes."

"Sure, Mel. See you later."

The day was still hot and humid. Mel's tank top clung to her skin. She thought about another shower but decided that a swim later in the day was a better idea. She couldn't settle to do her real estate licensing course. The encounter with Dono was too fresh and her nerves twanged with agitation and anger.

She had to decide how to handle Dono. She wasn't going to let him jeopardize Tyler's life. Somehow she would block his access to Ty. Threats of court action might keep him at bay for a while. But Dono was a person who had to win. He wouldn't let anyone keep him from what he wanted. And if anger was fuelled by the power of crystal meth …?

Mel settled into the cushioned chair. Soon the exhaustion of stress and sleepless nights caught up with her and she slept deeply.

☙

Joe and Devon changed into swim suits inside the cottage. Devon bet Joe he'd be the first one ducked. He wanted to wager for a painting position. The loser has to climb the ladder. Joe took the bet knowing that Devon would win and trying to picture Devon bouncing to music up on the ladder.

Everyone was in the water when Mel, Tyler and Edie came around the corner of the house and waved at them. Mel's face registered surprise at seeing Joe and another young person there. She pulled her shoulders into resignation. Joe recognized the feeling. He'd had it often these last two weeks.

Marion waved and came out of the water.

"Hi, Mel, Edie, Tyler. Let me get dried off and we'll sit on the deck." Marion hugged Tyler and made him shriek with the cold water.

"I brought my bathing suit," Mel said. "It's been such a hot day."

"You go ahead, Mel. I've got things covered here. C'mon, Ty. You can help me find paper plates. And you can help wash and cut some veggies."

Mel changed quickly and didn't linger on shore. She dove off the dock and swam underwater a long distance before surfacing. When she came up, she startled for a moment to see Devon treading water beside her.

"I kind of raced you. I wanted to see if I could swim on top of the water as fast as you could underwater," he said.

"Well, I think you're faster," Mel grinned. "Hi. I'm Mel. That was my son, Tyler, and my mother that came with me."

"Isn't Tyler going to swim?"

"Not today. He's been sick. He needs to rest today."

"Bummer," Devon murmured.

"Who are you?" Mel asked.

"Oh, Devon. That's my dad there," he said pointing out Joe. "His name's Joe." They kept treading water.

"Yeah. I knew him when we were kids. He saved me once. I was out too far on a rubber float and he rescued me."

"Doesn't that mean you're his slave or something? Like he owns you for life because he saved yours?"

"I sure hope not," Mel said.

"Oh, bummer," Devon replied. He grinned at Mel and kicked away towards shore in the undulating movements used by sea lions.

Marion and Edie had the deck table set with dinner when everyone came out of the water. A large pan of lasagna, crusty with melted cheese, sat in the centre of the table.

Joe settled beside Tyler and asked him about the hospital.

"Any pretty nurses there, Ty?"

"Nope. Mostly they're just mean. They made me pee in a bottle," he said.

"I see." Joe was nodding thoughtfully. "Doesn't do much for your image, does it?"

Tyler shook his head. "I saw an old man do that once. I'm only seven."

"Much too young," Joe agreed.

Tyler was staring at Devon, his eyes focusing on the piercing in his eyebrow.

"Can I touch that?" he asked Devon.

"The ring? Sure if you want to," Devon said.

Tyler's finger was tentative and he pulled back. "Does it hurt?" he asked.

"Nope. Once it got caught on the facecloth and pulled pretty bad."

"Yewh," Tyler said.

Jeremy and Richie were looking too with great interest. Scott raised his eyebrows at them as if to say don't-even-think-about-it.

Edie commented that she was ravenous and piled her plate with lasagna. She hadn't eaten much today.

"How come?" Richie asked.

"I was on a bus then went to visit somebody," she said.

"Didn't they feed you?" Jeremy piped in. "We always eat when we go visiting."

"No. He doesn't have a kitchen," Edie replied.

Mel looked at her, willing her to stop right here. Edie looked back, determination on her face that she would keep Owen real.

"We'd love to hear about your visit later, Edie," Scott said. "More conversation for us when the kids are off playing."

Edie took the hint and nodded. Mel let herself breathe again.

Joe was sitting across from Mel and watched the play of emotions on her face. The tension around the issue of her father obviously ran high. He wondered if she ever visited him. Probably not much different than with himself. Lots of anger and no wish to visit. Nathan couldn't tell him anything about the criminal case even if Joe wanted to ask. But he figured that Owen could. Whatever Mel knew made her angry. Joe couldn't blame her for that.

Joe sipped his wine and watched Mel. He noticed how gracefully she moved, not like some small people who speed-walked through life. Her hair was curling up as it dried after her swim and formed a soft golden frame for her face. Occasionally, she tucked stray strands behind her ears. She had such small hands, such delicate ears, he thought. She didn't look like a person who could handle a rough ride in life. She was far too pretty to be tough.

If Mel was aware of Joe's scrutiny she didn't let on to Joe. Sometimes Joe caught himself studying her too intently and looked away when she caught his eye. Would she have come if she'd known he'd be there? It wouldn't have stopped Joe, had he known. Why should she let him deprive her of an evening at the lake? After her stressful weekend with Tyler, and with Dono, she needed this relaxation. Besides, he really wasn't bothering her, wasn't throwing her family situation in her face. Not that he had any right to; his was as bad. Did that make him a victim too?

When did he start to think of himself as a victim? Probably ever since he knew he carried all the weight of the 30 years — that Nathan couldn't share the load or the blame.

Mel raised her chin and looked at Joe across from her. He smiled a weak smile. He could tell she was testing how he would react and not wanting to feel foolish if he rebuffed her. She smiled back. He didn't exactly look like an ogre. His skin was bronzed and the fair hairs on his arms glistened in the sun. He didn't look intimidating, in fact the opposite. She could see if she cared to take it in that he was gentle with Devon and Tyler. He and Dev had a relaxed relationship that came through in Devon's charming spirit. You can tell something about their parenting when you see how kids behave. Joe thought he was solid on that front.

"Hey, Dad," Devon said, bringing Joe out of his reverie. "Maybe somebody knows where there's a skateboarding park."

"Yeah, maybe." He looked around. "Dev brought his skateboard with him and he'd like to find a park to use it. Any suggestions?"

"Sure," Jeremy said. "I skateboard. Richie too. It's at the Skatepark on Corbould Street."

"You want to go sometime?" Devon asked. "Can we go, Dad?"

Joe looked at Jeremy then at Scott. Scott waited for Jeremy to respond.

"Nah. Not in the summer. We can do that when school starts.

Dad's going to get us stuff to build a raft. I'm trying to talk him into a boat instead. Just a punter, ya'know?" He looked at his father who nodded. "Can Devon help, Dad?"

"I don't see why not," Scott answered.

"Devon's helping me fix up his grandmother's house but we're not going to work all the time. I could bring him out here some times. If he wants to." He looked at Devon who seemed to be thinking it all over.

Joe turned to Mel. "Maybe Tyler would like to come with us some time. If it's all right with you."

Mel recognized the olive branch. "If he wants to," she said.

"Yeaahh!" said Tyler.

"What are you doing at the house?" Edie asked.

"It needs painting and some repairs to the porches and garage. She's selling it when we're finished and going to an assisted living building."

"Yeah," Devon said, "Gram had a stroke and needs some help. But I help her. She's great." He looked at his father. "Hey, maybe she could come out and watch us build the raft, or boat, or whatever."

Joe wasn't prepared for that. "Well ... I don't know Dev. Look at the stairs here."

"But she could sit on the deck where we are. There's only one step in the back. She could come in through the house." He suddenly realized he was offering hospitality at Scott and Marion's house and shouldn't do it. "Oh, sorry."

"That's okay, Devon. I think if your grandmother is well enough to come and sit here for a while that it would be nice for her. We don't mind at all. Joe? Is it possible?"

Joe hesitated. This was moving too fast for him.

"Well, we had her out for an ice cream today. She managed. I'll ask her. See what she thinks."

"Hey! Let's take Ty up back and see if the rabbits are there."

The other two scrambled to follow Jeremy and suddenly the deck was silent.

"So," Edie said looking at Joe. "Your mother's on her own?" Joe nodded. He's sure Edie must know what had happened to Nathan.

"Women seem to get left holding the bag," Edie continued. "Although, some people choose it. To be alone, I mean." She looked at Mel. "Some times it's the best choice."

"I've wondered," Joe said, "why my mother didn't choose it years ago."

"Maybe she did make the best choice," Mel offered. "Staying." Joe looked at her curiously. "I mean, it's hard being a single parent. And for a woman 30 years ago, even harder."

"I can't understand staying in a situation that is humiliating and degrading," Joe said.

"That's because you're a man," said Mel. "You have a sister, right?" she asked. Joe nodded. "So she had two kids to raise. Who's to say you weren't better off having a comfortable house and food on the table. You've done all right. Became a pilot. What about your sister?"

"She's… well educated. Lives in Australia."

"Women will suffer a lot to provide for their kids," Mel finished.

"So you're saying she might have stayed because of me?" He was incredulous.

"And your sister. Kids come first with many women. Certainly before their own happiness."

"Not to be too personal," Joe continued, "but you left your husband."

"Yeah. But I reasoned that Tyler and I were better off *without* him." Tears came to her eyes and she hung her head. "And now it's even more important that I keep Tyler away from him."

"What's happening, Mel?" Scott asked.

Mel pulled herself together. "Tyler had his asthmatic attack because of a fight Dono had with Allison. I've talked to her. She left about 10 o'clock after fighting with Dono. Dono found Tyler on the floor in distress shortly after that. Tyler says they were fighting and he got scared." Mel took a deep breath. She looked at Scott. "The doctor said it was a close call. I can't risk having Ty stay with Dono again. So, now I have to find a way to keep Tyler from him."

"You can get a court order," Scott said.

"I've already threatened Dono with that. I think it'll work for a while but it's not the solution."

"The solution is for Dono to go to jail," Edie declared.

Mel put her hand on Edie's arm. "Mum."

"Well, it's time some one did something. He's dangerous. We know that."

Mel looked at the others, clearly embarrassed that so much had been said that revealed her problems. Joe avoided her eyes and wondered if it was time to check on the kids or go to the bathroom.

"Well, he at least should be investigated again in the fraud case," Edie added. She looked at Joe. "I don't see why my husband and your father have to carry all the blame. I'm sure Dono was mixed up in it."

Joe leaned forward. Now it involved *his* life. "How do you mean?" he said.

"Only that he has a criminal mind and he intimidates people. He lives large. Buys expensive things."

Edie glanced at Mel to see how ticked off Mel was about how she was talking. Mel was looking thoughtful.

"Well," Mel said, "since we're talking about this, I talked to Allison. Dono hurt her. Hit her and caused enough damage that she had an x-ray. That's what I'd use in court, as well as Ty's hospitalization, to keep him away from Ty." No one said anything, so she continued. "Ty heard the words 'I'll tell'. Allison said them. Then when I saw Allison at the bus station today — she left town today — she said she couldn't deal with accounts and stuff anymore." Mel swallowed. She looked at her mother. "I'll bet there's something there."

"Maybe the Crown Counsel hasn't looked deep enough," Scott said. "Maybe they didn't have enough probable cause for warrants." He leaned with elbows on his knees, thinking.

"So — what do I do?" Mel asked." "Do I go back to the Crown Counsel with this information?"

"Yeah, I think so," Scott said. Joe was nodding his head. "If they think it's important enough, they'll follow it up and find Allison. I'll go with you if you like," Scott told her.

"Why don't I go with her?" Joe said. "It involves me and my family too." He looked at Mel whose eyes told him she was thinking that offer through. "I have more time on my hands than you do," he told Scott.

Mel began nodding her head. Joe really wasn't any threat. "Okay," she said.

By this time the kids could be heard in the back yard kicking a soccer ball around. Mel felt she had to get Tyler and go home before he got too worked up. The women gathered belongings and dishes and went indoors.

Joe and Scott were silent for a few minutes. Joe broke the silence.

"She really has a load to carry doesn't she?"

"Yeah, it's a bitch," Scott said softly. "This isn't the first time Edie's talked about Dono that way. It rattles Mel, I think because she agrees but feels stuck. What can she do about it? She's told me a number of times that she doesn't know anything about Dono's business. At least now, maybe there's someone else who can give some information."

"And maybe Edie would ease up about Owen if she could spread the guilt," Joe said.

"That too," Scott agreed and settled into the deck chair.

Joe nursed his wine and thought about how complex families could be.

· Chapter 7 ·

The next morning, Joe and Devon finished the painting at the back of the house. Joe started adding up the supplies he still had to buy. He added a new toilet seat to the list and washers to fix taps in bathroom and kitchen. Over lunch they made afternoon plans.

"What do you think, Dev? You want to skateboard for a while then maybe go to the water park?"

"Yeah! Are you going to swim too?" Devon's face was eager.

"Well… it could happen, I guess." Joe grinned. "But don't expect me to skateboard," he said.

"Well… if you don't want to, okay. But if Gram beats you at skateboarding, you're going to feel like a wimp." Devon's mouth twitched with a smile.

Joe gave him a startled look. "You're kidding. Right?"

Devon and Vera laughed. "Gotcha," Devon said.

They tidied the kitchen and Vera went to the living room for her nap. Joe took their bathing suits from the drying spot on the front porch and found two towels while Devon collected his skateboard and iPod.

In the car Joe arranged to leave Devon at the Skatepark while he went shopping for repair supplies. Since this had taken less than an hour, he stopped at Scott's office to talk to Mel about seeing the Crown Counsel. She was in the middle of a phone call when he arrived.

"Hi," she said. Her eyes shifted with uncertainty, then, she looked back.

"Hi," Joe said. "I thought we should arrange a time to go to the prosecutor's office."

"You know, you really don't have to do this," Mel said.

"Well, I'm not thrilled about getting involved with this but … it would be best to have more information… and if it would help you.… Neither of my parents can tell me anything about what happened. My mother doesn't seem to know, or won't say what she knows. And my father can't. Did you know he's in a dementia unit?"

"I heard something, yeah." Mel looked at him uneasily.

Joe was silent. Unsure how much more he wanted to say. "It's a nightmare. He doesn't know anybody and can't do anything for himself."

"Maybe he's not suffering if he doesn't know what's going on. Maybe being in prison is more punishment than that."

"Oh, I think this is a very special prison," Joe said quietly. He pulled back to the reason for his visit. "So, when do you think we should see the Crown Counsel?"

"Why don't I phone now and see when he's free," Mel said. Joe nodded.

Mel made the call and arranged to be there immediately after work. Joe said he'd be back around five.

"Where's Devon?" Mel asked.

"I left him at the Skatepark and then we're going to the water-park. Ever been there?"

"To the water-park, yes. It was a couple of years ago. Tyler mainly stayed in the shallow pools."

"Well, if it seems good and Devon wants to go back, maybe

you'd let us take Tyler one day." Maybe Joe was pushing it but he wondered just how far Mel had come in relaxing her hard-edged feelings about him.

"I ... guess. I worry when he's not with me." Mel was thoughtful. "I'd have to go over with you how and when to use his inhaler. He's good about it, and he did his best that night with Dono, but you'd need to know in case exercise tips him into distress. He's supposed to use it before exercise now, too."

"That's got to be really rough, having to monitor his activities like that."

"We get by. If I can limit Dono's influence in his life it would be a help."

"The stress of it, you mean?"

"Pretty much, yeah."

"Well, maybe that will work out too if the prosecutor does something." Joe found himself wondering what Mel's face would look like without worry lines. She was pretty, even when stressed. She'd had just enough sun to give her cheeks that sun-kissed glow. With a bit of joy in her life she would be beautiful. He felt himself melt a bit inside, go a bit liquid. Must be the heat. "Okay, I'll take off and be back around 5 o'clock."

∽

When Joe picked Devon up at the Skatepark, Devon talked nonstop about the turns and jumps he was mastering. Joe could see Devon's excitement and marvelled at the intensity of adolescent feelings.

"Why do you like skateboarding," Joe asked. "What is it about it that thrills you?"

"Are you kidding, Dad? It's almost like flying. You're really out there but have some control, as much as your own skill allows. I know the guys who get really good feel like they're king of the hill."

Joe saw the parallels to any sport or risk-taking behaviour. Walking on the edge and daring to either fall off or win. It was a good thing, he thought, channelling teen energy that way. What was his flying, after all, but risk-taking. He thought of it as a guy-thing.

"Next time we come here I'll stay and watch," Joe said.

"Way cool," Devon replied.

At the water-park, Devon raced Joe to the slides, convincing Joe that if you didn't do it immediately you'd chicken out. Joe didn't chicken out. After two hours they were exhausted and sat with sandwiches and sodas in the shade.

"This is great," Joe said. "We never had anything like this when we were kids."

"Yeah, but, you had the lake. It's fun," Devon said.

"It was the most fun," Joe said. "It was carefree, you know? Every day was an adventure."

"Just like this afternoon. We didn't have to think about work or Grandma being sick."

"Yeah, like balancing your life out. Some fun, some serious." He looked a Devon. "That's important, not leaning too heavily towards one side of life. Right?"

"Sure, sure, Dad." Devon looked thoughtful. "I'm glad we're not just painting," he grinned.

"Me too," Joe said.

"But Gram needs help, doesn't she?"

"Unfortunately, yes."

"So she's going to live in a hospital, or something?"

"Not quite. There are living spaces where people can have their own room but there's nursing help too. Not so much like a hospital because they can have easy chairs and TV's and decorate their rooms however they like. Like a small apartment. Some one cooks their meals and does their laundry, that kind of thing."

"I wish some one would do my laundry and cook my meals," Devon grinned.

"You mean they don't?"

"Mom's trying to make me to do stuff. Says I have to learn to look after myself."

"That's okay. It has to happen some day. Better to know before you're living on your own."

"I guess." Devon didn't sound convinced.

"Do you know the first time I cooked Kraft Dinner by myself I nearly set the place on fire?"

"Really?" Devon was astounded.

"Yes, really. You know how it says to add butter after the noodles are cooked?" Devon nodded. "I figured you had to melt the butter first. How could you mix a blob of hard butter into the noodles? So I got out a frying pan and turned the element on high. The butter caught on fire." Devon gasped. "The flames were three feet tall and licking at the fan. Then I stupidly carried the burning pan, flames and all, to the sink and ran water on it. It spluttered and spit something awful. I'm lucky I didn't burn myself along with destroying the house."

Devon's eyes were wide.

"That's why you need to learn to look after yourself. It's survival."

"Wow," Devon said.

"Now, I like ordering in a pizza. Much safer," Joe said with a straight face.

"I agree," said Devon dead-panned. "I'm always going to keep a list of pizza restaurant numbers handy. Much safer."

෨

Devon was using the parking lot at the Court House for skateboarding while he waited for Joe and Mel who were inside. The asphalt was broken in places which gave him challenges that he liked.

A woman coming across the lot stopped at her car a few feet from Devon. She looked up as her key opened the car door and stopped, staring at Devon. Devon stopped too, wondering if he was in trouble for skateboarding here.

"Is it okay if I skateboard here? I'm just waiting for my dad. Don't mean to get in the way of anything," Devon said.

"I don't care if you skateboard. I just thought for a moment that I knew you."

"I don't live here, but my dad used to. Maybe you know him? Joe Bennett?"

"So that's why you're familiar. Sure I knew Joe. We were neighbours. So, is he back to stay or for a visit?"

"Just a visit. My grandma had a stroke and we're helping her."

"Oh." She paused. "Well, tell him Elena said hello. I miss being back-fence neighbours. Perhaps I'll see him when I visit my mother." She winked as she left.

Joe and Mel were coming across the parking lot, grim looks on their faces.

"He acted like I was trying to nail Dono out of revenge," Mel was saying.

"He sure wasn't giving much credit to the information. But he did say he would try to talk to Allison," Joe was thoughtful.

"I wonder if he'll even try to find her. Probably wait for her to be beaten up or something."

Joe agreed with Mel's cynical interpretation of the meeting. Yet, he could understand that the authorities didn't have a lot go on. You simply can't search some one's private space without justifiable cause.

"Hi, Dad." Devon flipped his skateboard into his arms. "I talked to some one who knows you."

"Yeah? Who?"

"She said to say hello from Elena and that she missed being your back-fence neighbour."

"Oh." Joe stopped still. She actually remembered him. The famous and the infamous all registered in memory.

"Do you remember her?"

"Yeah, she's hard to forget."

Mel looked at him quizzically. "But better forgotten," Joe murmured. "I'll drop you at home?" he asked Mel. She shook her head. "My car's at the office."

"Right." Joe said, clearly distracted.

Joe was silent delivering Mel to her car. Bur Devon made up for it.

"Are we going to see you again, Mel?" Devon asked. "And Tyler too," he added.

"Well, sure. But I think your dad has some things to do. Um, thanks, Joe, for coming with me today." She turned away.

"Mel … we'd like to see you again. I'd like to. Can we arrange something with the boys?"

"Okay." She paused. "I'll think about it. Bye."

At home, Vera was finishing her Meals-On-Wheels. The fruit cup was left untouched.

"Hey, Gram," Devon said, "Dad's going to show me how to make Kraft Dinner."

Vera looked at him, then at Joe, and burst out laughing. "You didn't think it was funny when I was eleven," Joe accused, a smile twitching his lips.

Vera waved Joe away and said she would show Devon how to make it.

"Suits me," Joe laughed and went out to sit on the back porch. He could hear pans rattling and water running in the kitchen.

He eased back on the top step. The back fence loomed into his line of vision. Elena Crossini — back-fence neighbours. Did she really remember it like that? Like we were all friends together?

'Good fences make good neighbours?' Not likely. It was just her way of sliding over the harsh facts of her behaviour. Maybe her life has been so filled with sexual escapades that meant nothing to her that she doesn't remember what it did to his family. Her affair with Nathan caused such horrendous events to follow, how could she not be aware of them?

The Back Fence. He felt like it should be capitalized. In those days it didn't stand for much, didn't keep Elena from slipping around its edges and into the garage. Elena was always back there, out of sight and waiting.

Although, not always out of sight. He remembered being drawn to the fence by the scent of suntan lotion, and, maybe something else, if he let himself think about it. She would come to the fence-line and talk to him, when she was sunbathing in a skimpy bikini, with the neck strings undone and the small pieces of fabric barely clinging to her breasts. And then with her dark hair, shiny as polished mahogany and falling in waves to her shoulders, she'd flip it back with a casually seductive movement that shifted her bathing suit top, allowing one large, pink nipple to pucker in the air. With 15-year-old Joe looking on, transfixed, she'd make an ineffectual tug at the collapsed cup and demurely mouth an apology.

Back then he couldn't look at her without thinking about his father touching her. He would stand there clenching his fists in anger and confusion ... and ... sometimes with a tight feeling in his jeans. He remembered he couldn't move of his own volition, just stood there until she turned away and loosened her hold on him.

No, no, she didn't stir sexual feelings in him, that wasn't what happened. How could he want her when his father was banging her, when she was destroying his family? That would be a betrayal of ... of decency.

Joe inhaled deeply trying to shake off the disturbing images. No, he thought, he really couldn't have a clear picture of what happened 30 years ago, not with so many emotions still swirling around. He couldn't be sure about his feelings when he was fifteen or sixteen. That time was all a mystery anyway, clouded by hormones, bootlegged beer and the occasional hit from a joint being passed around.

Joe dropped his shoulders and breathed out; he'd been sitting there tense as a tightrope. He opened his fists and saw crescent indentations from his nails. He had to let it go, but doubted he could until this yard was no longer part of his life.

"Dad, Dad," Devon called. "KD's ready."

He got up, grateful for the reprieve from toxic memories, and went inside.

· Chapter 8 ·

↣

The downtown shopping area was congested with summer visitors. Slowed cars were looking for mapped destinations, heads swiveling and peering at storefront signs.

Edie groaned in frustration, hit the steering wheel with the heel of her hand. Tyler turned sharply to look at her.

"What's wrong, Grandma?"

"Oh, nothing, I guess. The traffic's so slow and the car's so hot. That's all."

"There's Safeway. We're almost there," Tyler said.

A car flashed past them as they entered the parking lot. Edie had a notion it was Dono but didn't tell Tyler who seemed well recovered from his rough weekend. Their shopping only took a few minutes and, when they came out, Dono was slouched against Edie's car, a cigarette glowing from his fingers.

"Hi, Ty. Glad to see you looking good." Dono glanced at Edie and could see the tight line that was her mouth. Edie told him to put out the cigarette around Tyler. Didn't he have enough breathing problems without his father adding to them.

Dono threw the cigarette to the ground and stomped on it. He was ticked-off at Edie being right.

Tyler stared up at Dono, uncertainty on his face. Edie looked at

Tyler and saw his fear. The hospital visit was still a vivid memory.

Dono crouched down to Tyler's eye level.

"We'll get together again soon, Ty." Tyler just kept looking and blinking. He reached for Edie's hand and leaned into her.

"It's okay, Ty, no need to be scared." Dono took both of Tyler's hands in his. Edie stepped forward with one foot as if to stop Dono getting any closer to his son.

"Just stay out of this, Edie. I have rights. More than a grandmother."

"You won't have them for long," Edie declared.

"Stay out of my way, Edie. You don't want to get hurt." Tyler backed away from Dono, pulled his hands back to his sides.

"See what you're doing? You're turning my son against me. You want that to happen, don't you?" Dono accused. His voice carried over the parking lot. Other shoppers turned their heads and halted to see what was happening.

"I don't have to turn him against you. You do a good job of that on your own," Edie hissed. She grabbed Tyler's arm and pulled him behind her, shielding him from whatever Dono might do next.

"I won't stand for it, Edie. I'll make Mel live up to the custody agreement."

"Do whatever you like, Dono. But keep in mind that we know what you did to Allison and we'll use it against you in court."

Shock and anger played across Dono's face. "So, Allison ran to you with some outrageous story did she?" Dono pulled up straight and leaned into Edie's face. "Nobody screws me around, not since I was ten years old."

"Is that why you don't mind screwing around a seven-year-old? You learned young so your son needs to learn the same lesson and damn the consequences? Hit a woman while your son listens and learns how to solve problems with his fists?" By now Edie was practically shrieking. Tyler was trembling, hanging onto Edie's leg. A circle of bystanders had gathered and were watching the drama. People murmured but nobody moved to get involved. Dono suddenly became aware of the audience.

"This isn't over," he threatened, then jumped into his car and was gone.

Edie hugged Tyler. "You all right, Sweetie?" His breathing was rapid but quiet. Edie put him in the car and let him settle. A tear slid down his cheek.

"Oh, Tyler, I'm so sorry. I didn't mean to upset you." She gently brushed the tear away with her thumb. "Sometimes your dad, well, he gets me going and ... I should carry duct tape with me, you know, like Red Green, and whenever I start to mouth off you can wrap my mouth in it. Just keep going around and around until I look like a mummy." Edie pantomimed being wrapped around her head like she was using a lasso. Tyler's eyes widened and he grinned. Edie hugged him again, said, sorry Sweetie, and got in the car.

෴

Joe and Devon had a work pattern—three hours of work and an afternoon of play. Within three days two sides of the house were painted and repaired. What tools weren't available in the garage, Joe borrowed from Scott and Marco. Devon absorbed the lessons on cutting angles with a mitre box and setting nails and filling the holes for a smooth finish.

Occasionally Vera came to the porch and watched them. Beside the back door was a tomato plant in a pot. It had tiny green tomatoes on it. Vera watered it every day. Joe had asked Vera where it came from. Marika was the reply.

While Vera seemed to focus on the plant or Devon, the garage loomed large for Joe. He couldn't stop himself wondering how much she thought about Nathan's visits to the garage to meet Elena. Joe hoped that with the passing of years, and Nathan and

Elena each living elsewhere, that the memory was no longer constant, was dimming enough to give her peace.

Not that he had seen any evidence of these memories during his stay here. Vera didn't talk about them and he had no way of knowing what had happened during the thirty years he was away. And that opened a whole new line of thinking. What had happened after he left? What had been said between his mother and father? Had they fought? Had he begged forgiveness? Did she extract promises? Or did nothing happen? Maybe Nathan continued to see Elena clandestinely or even openly. Maybe Vera kept on as she had begun, silent and closed in. He'd been thinking about her as passive and stoic, but maybe not. He had left and shut the door on his family's life. All he had were 30-year-old memories, a rusted, twisted heap of battered truths.

Sandra. Sandra was here for a few years after he left. Not many, that's true. But she'd have some notion of the emotional tone of the house in those years. At some point he would talk to her about it.

Joe looked over at his mother, sitting on a hard kitchen chair in the middle of the porch, her cane, standing on its four feet, beside her. Her face was raised to the sun and she appeared to be drinking it in, absorbing heat and life from the sun's rays. Brown age spots on her wrinkled skin spoke of decades of living. Her frame was shrunken and bony and displayed none of the softening roundness of healthy muscle. She was a life in decline, sliding with some speed towards death, but putting on some breaks with the invigorating effects of ultra violet light.

How long do you keep reaching forward, trying to grab hold of life instead of allowing the easier slippage to carry you down? What do you have to have inside you to keep you wanting more life events that risk the heartache of loss and disillusionment, that bear witness to your own collapse? Joe didn't think he'd care that much about living if ever he reached his mother's age and disabled state.

Devon had finished staining the ends of the boards that would repair the skirting on the porch. Joe had explained that the ends wouldn't rot as fast if they were sealed before they were nailed in place. He was surprised and pleased with how eagerly Devon was learning the many small tasks of general repairs.

Joe had started thinking about this time with Devon as a time for learning survival skills. A person sure needed something to help them over rough patches in life. Any skills or accomplishments could only add to self-confidence and make any problem easier to handle. This time with him was turning into a lucky break. *He'd* been lucky, in a way. The Air Force had propped him up and had given him a life filled with structure and built-in problem-solvers. Then he'd left the service and had to fly on his own. He thought he was coping.

"Gram," Devon said.

Vera turned towards his voice and raised her hand to shield her eyes.

"Gram, I need something to drink. How about you? Dad?"

Vera and Joe each nodded. "What do you think, Devon? Just water or should I go for something else?" Joe was thinking he could pick up beer and the something else was for them. "How 'bout I go for some iced tea? Or I could bring back a slushie for each of you," he offered.

"Yeah, a grape slushie. How about you, Gram?" Vera's eyes widened. "Try a lemon-lime, Gram. It's kind of regal sounding. I'll bet when the Queen has a slushie she has lemon-lime." Devon grinned. Vera nodded and smiled.

"I'll bring iced tea too. For another time," Joe said.

When Joe returned from his drinks run he had a fistful of brochures. He fanned them at Devon and Vera.

"Let's see what the tourists do in Chilliwack." Devon crowded beside him on the sofa and read along with Joe. Devon turned thumbs down on museums and gardens. Joe agreed to bicycle tour that used the rail bed of the old Kettle Valley railway and a return to the water slides if Devon would go fishing with him one day.

"What about fishing equipment? Is there any here?" Devon asked.

"I'll check the garage, but if not, I'll buy some. We can leave it with Scott for letting us enjoy his cottage."

Devon thought they should find an activity for Gram. She nodded agreement when Joe suggested Minter Gardens. It was advertised as wheelchair-friendly. Vera said she could ask Janet, her Home Support Aide, about a wheel chair. Devon retracted his ban on gardens since it was for Gram.

Devon and Vera slurped their slushies, each trying to outdo the other with the loudest slurp. Once, Vera choked and took several minutes to settle. Joe held his breath until she recovered.

By the time they were done, Vera was ready for a nap and Devon was ready for some fun.

"Let's explore some of the other swimming areas," Joe suggested. "There are rivers and lakes all around here." They packed their gear adding beer for Joe and iced tea for Devon.

They travelled south until they hit Chilliwack Lake Road then followed the lake shore until they saw a family swimming and decided that was good enough endorsement. They spent two hours power-swimming then treaded water to see who could last the longest. Joe let Devon win.

Devon had the iPod plugged into his ears and wasn't prepared when Joe suddenly braked the car. "Whoa!" Devon said. He looked around. "How come we stopped?"

"Look over there, at that sign." Joe pointed to a sign board advertising sailing lessons. "Wow," he said. "Think about it. Sailing lessons. Let's go ask about them." Joe was out of the car first and headed across the lot. He was inside the office before Devon reached the door.

"Hello, folks." A darkly tanned man, grey-haired, about sixty years old approached Joe with his hand outstretched. He wore tan shorts, ragged around the bottom, a T-shirt advertising Kokanee beer and navy canvas boat shoes which were no longer new. "How are you folks today? You local or just passing through?"

"Here for a while this summer," Joe answered, taking his hand. "Just saw your sign and wanted to ask about lessons."

"Really?' Devon's reaction was part surprise and part glee. "Can we really sail?" he asked.

"Sure, son, if your dad wants to try. I'm Sam Bailey. My wife and I run this business."

"What's involved with lessons?" Joe asked.

"We don't teach Canadian Yachting Association Certification. What we do here is just the basics for sailing for fun in small vessels on lakes. You don't need to be able to read charts, tide tables or that sort of thing. And it's any number of lessons you want until you feel comfortable."

"Can we have a look at the boats you use?"

"Sure. Right this way."

The trio walked a short distance to the water's edge. Two small sail boats were tied to the dock, blue bumpers squeaking with the soft movement against the wooden decking.

"This one is a Walker Bay ten-footer. Great for young people. Easy to keep under control, safe and stable. The other one is the X-Boat. At sixteen feet it's big enough for two sailors. Of course we provide life jackets and Aileen or I go out with anyone still training."

Joe looked at Devon who nodded his head vigorously. "What about your experience," Joe asked.

"Both Aileen and I are CYA certified. Our papers are in the office. We've sailed around here for 30 odd years. Lakes and ocean. This is kind of retirement for us."

"I think you've got two new recruits," Joe smiled.

"Yes!" Devon punched the air.

Joe and Devon talked excitedly about sailing on the way home. Devon burst into the house calling to Vera, eager to relay their great news.

The house was silent. The TV sat in darkness. Vera's pillow and light afghan lay crumpled on the sofa. Devon called Gram, Gram as he ran to the kitchen.

"She's not here! Where is she? He stopped and looked at Joe. "Dad?"

Joe went to the back door and scanned the yard. Vera's hard chair still sat on the porch. There was no sign of her.

"Where can she be, Dad? She can't go anywhere by herself." Devon was clearly shaken, his eyes watery and searching.

Joe rubbed his face. "Yes. Yes she can." He had forgotten it was Thursday.

"Dev, she's all right. It's Thursday."

"What is that supposed to mean?"

"On Thursdays she goes to see Nathan, your grandfather. On a special bus that picks her up. I forgot."

"How could you forget that? Why didn't I know about my grandfather? Where is he?"

"He's in a home for old people who aren't well and need care."

"Like Gram's going to be?"

"Sort of. But different too. He doesn't remember things. He isn't safe to live on his own."

"Like Alzheimer's or something?"

"Yeah, like that."

"Why didn't you tell me? How could you not let me know about my grandfather?"

"Well, there are problems. I …."

"You never let me see him all these years. Nobody mentions him! I thought he must be dead and now I discover I have a grandfather!" Devon had become strident, his face red and eyes teary with emotion. "Both Gram and Grandpa need help. I've been here five days and you didn't mention him!" Devon slammed out the door into the back yard.

Joe slumped into a chair. This had been handled badly. He should have found a way to introduce the subject but it was easier not to. He was having enough trouble dealing with it himself never mind trying to explain it to a 14-year-old. Joe pulled a beer from the fridge and iced tea for Devon and took them outside. Devon had his head resting on his arms and cradled in his lap. Joe sat beside him on the step. He silently offered the drink. Devon wiped his face and accepted it.

"I don't understand. Why didn't you tell me about Grandpa? Even Gram hasn't said anything. It's not fair."

"Dev ... there were problems. That's why I left home when I was young."

"But that doesn't mean you just forget about your parents and not help them when they need it." Dev started flicking his brow piercing with his right hand.

"Well, sometimes it does. Things can get so bad between people that they don't want to be around each other any more."

"What could be so bad that you don't help your parents when they get sick? How fair is that?" Devon was still agitated and wasn't going to be brushed off.

"We're here helping Grandma. We'll help her get into her new place and sell the house. Grandpa's being looked after in his care facility. Everything will work out fine, Dev."

"Maybe they needed you when you weren't here," Devon said quietly. He looked into Joe's eyes. "And you weren't there for them."

Joe put his arm across his son's shoulders and drew him against him.

"Maybe they did," he said

· Chapter 9 ·

Over the next two days the quiet of the house was heavy with disappointment. It weighted every listless movement and wan smile. Joe and Devon continued to paint and Devon followed Joe's instructions. But each time their eyes met, Joe could see hurt he had caused. Devon's accusation, "It's not fair!" repeated in his head. Joe withdrew into his regret. He felt the gap between them and didn't know how to set things right.

Devon spent time sitting alone on the back porch, his iPod plugged in, the piercing an easy target for his unsettled body. Occasionally he would slip into the hollow beside his grandmother on the sofa and lay his head on her shoulder. He talked quietly to her and she'd smile at him, trying to draw his grin, aware of the changed behaviour and wondering what had happened. She looked at Joe with concern but he offered no answers. Once, a tear, unfelt by enervated muscles, sat on her cheek and declared her loss.

Devon spoke his disappointment in Joe with every averted glance and, when Joe caught Devon's eye, he could read the message — the respect Devon had had for him was shaken. Here he was thinking he was going to add to Devon's sense of confidence, give him skills for facing the tough times in life. Instead, he'd created confusion about responsibility and neglect. What a shitty way to parent, he thought.

It wasn't until they had their first sailing lesson on Saturday that Devon's dispirited affect lifted. Sailing with Aileen in the small boat, Devon caught on quickly to using the rudder. The breeze was just heavy enough to move the craft but soft enough not to cause anxiety. Devon could see how the sails caught the wind and pushed the boat along. He found he could control the direction they went. The sense of mastery thrilled him. By the end of the first lesson he was hooked.

Joe relaxed into the quietness of the water and felt like he could drift on the lake forever. The shoreline slid by, tranquil and cool, allowing Joe to shove aside the emotional issues at home. He loved the control he had in the boat. He could change direction at will and it was peaceful. He could tell that the tension that had spiked in the last few days was losing its edge.

He'd been a fool not to tell Devon about his grandfather. What was he thinking? Of course, Devon would learn about Nathan and ask questions. He should have been prepared for that. It had been cowardice, sheer cowardice, he realized, protecting his own feelings by not tackling the issue head on.

Well, what was done was done. He was glad to see Devon smile again. They needed to talk about Nathan's dementia before Devon met him. And he'd certainly meet him. Devon was insistent and Joe couldn't see how to talk him out of it.

After their lesson Joe stood in line at the Safeway deli. It was far too nice and too hot to think of cooking at home. A barbequed chicken would fill their supper needs. Suddenly, Tyler was at his side.

"Hi, Joe," he said. "We're shopping too." He looked around. "Where's Devon?"

Joe pointed to the pastry section and Tyler took off. Mel hurried behind him. "Tyler!" she called.

"Oh, hi, Mel," Joe said. "Ty's okay. Devon's over there."

"I guess we all have the same idea," she said, inclining her head at the prepared food.

"Then it's probably a good one," Joe answered.

"I think so. No cooking happening at my place, anyway."

Joe tipped his head towards Tyler. "How's he doing?"

"It's been a good week. Mum keeps him when I work and he's been fine."

They got in line behind all the other customers seeking relief from the kitchen.

"How is your mother?" Mel asked. "Heat's pretty hard on old people."

"She's managing. The bedroom side is shaded so nights are tolerable."

Devon had an enthralled Tyler listening to every word about the sailing lesson. Then Tyler said, "Wow, and you could make it go?" Mel saw Tyler's rapt expression and felt an instant liking for Devon, and made an instant decision.

Mel and Joe had each reached the front of the line. Mel turned to him.

"Are you and Devon eating alone?"

"Yeah. My mother gets meals prepared by her Home Support or Meals-on-Wheels. We haven't made a habit of having a regular mealtime with her."

"Well, why don't you bring your deli to my house. Give Devon and Tyler some more time together."

Joe couldn't believe his good luck. Not only might this break the gloomy spell at *his* house but he could actually spend time with attractive, caring, sweetly feminine Mel.

"That'd be great. I'll wait for you at the checkout and you can lead the way," Joe suggested.

"Where are we going, Dad?"

"Mel invited us to her house. We'll pool our take-out and sit in the yard."

Joe followed Mel's car, taking pleasure in the thought of spending time with her. Devon was silent but swivelled his head to look as they passed through this new area of the city. As they approached Mel's place Joe had to park at the curb. There was only room for one car in the driveway.

With Joe's mind now attuned to home repairs, he immediately noticed the maintenance needs as they stopped in front of the house. Joe could see that the aluminum siding was paint-chipped and dented in places that couldn't be explained. Shingles curled on the roof. The porch needed paint and some nails to secure loose boards.

Tyler bounded out of the car and opened the front door for Devon. "Come on and see my room. I've got lots of neat stuff. But Spider-man is still at my dad's. I asked him to bring it back."

The boys were gone before shopping bags could be unloaded. They burst into the house, startling Edie in the hallway. Edie held the door open as Mel and Joe brought in the groceries.

Edie stood in the hallway. "This is a surprise," she said, her tone both sarcastic and incredulous.

"For us too, Edie," Joe said. "Mel graciously offered to pool her dinner with ours. Lead me to the kitchen and I'll drop this load."

While Mel went outdoors to ready the eating area, Joe passed by the living room and noticed piles of books on the floor. No extra space here, that was certain. The rest of the downstairs had simply been neglected. The ceilings were peeling with effects of dampness. The lino was worn through in patches. The beautiful, huge dining furniture loomed over the area, speaking volumes about losses. The place was a disaster and, as far as Joe was concerned, should probably be bulldozed. How could a man allow his family to live like this? On the other hand, Mel was refusing help. Was that from stubborn pride or rigid integrity?

Tyler and Devon came out of Tyler's bedroom, each carrying a remote-controlled toy vehicle. Tyler clutched a Nascar racer and Devon held a big-tread crawler. Devon lifted his eyebrows in a how-about-this-for-fun fashion. Joe grinned back. A little regression couldn't be a bad thing. The boys found some sticks and rocks to construct a challenging race site. Within seconds Tyler's car was in the lead. Joe watched them from the doorway.

"They didn't take long to adjust, did they?" Mel stood behind Joe, peering around his shoulder at the boys. Joe liked her closeness. He could feel the heat of her body. And there was something citrus about her hair, a freshness that made him want to breathe deeply, or lick his lips. Or her lips? He didn't want to move. He didn't want the moment to end.

She passed around him, touching his arm to clear the way. Her hands balanced butter, cutlery and napkins. He pushed himself forward.

"Here. Let me take some things," he said.

Edie put chairs around the picnic table, saying nothing. When she glanced at Joe, he could tell there was some kind of tally going on in her mind. Guilt by association? That's what Mel had done. She seemed to have softened that stance. Complicity? What did he know and wasn't telling?

"Joe? How about a beer? Or wine? I've got both." Mel spoke from the kitchen doorway. He looked up, realized Edie was still aware of his every move.

"A beer. Thanks."

"Like father, like son," Edie said.

"Pardon?" Joe spun around to Edie's voice.

"Nothing. I just remembered that your father always drank beer. At barbeques, picnics. You know."

"Actually, I don't remember much of that. I was too busy doing damage control."

Edie had her hands braced on her hips. "Haven't we all been," she said.

Joe could feel the free-floating animosity. "I don't know about you," he said, "but mine started when I was a kid."

"Maybe you should have stuck around and finished the job."

"You can't stop a steamroller. The result's the same even if you try to stop it."

"Not everyone gets knocked down the first time around." Edie clutched her arms around her chest. "*With help*, some destruction could have been avoided."

Joe didn't want this to escalate. He retreated. "You're right, I wasn't here. But that doesn't mean anything would have changed. I fought my father ... I fought him," he finished softly.

"Mum!" Mel appeared through the door. "Stop trying to make scapegoats out of everyone. Joe is our guest. Leave him alone."

"I'm not burying my head in the sand," Edie replied. "There's more to this than anyone knows." She turned on her heel and went indoors.

"I'm sorry." Mel and Joe said it in unison.

"No, really, I'm sorry," Mel said quickly. "She ... she can't get her mind around the fact that her husband's in jail and guilty as sin."

"It's hard ... for me too. Just because Nathan isn't in jail doesn't mean I dismiss his guilt." He paused. "In fact, I'm very sure he's guilty as charged." Joe looked to Mel for some understanding gesture. She seemed to be waiting for him to say more. "I wasn't here and I have other issues with him. My mother can't, or doesn't, say anything."

"Even before her stroke?"

"When I'd visit with her she was like a carefree school kid. Time away from home. Excited about what I could show her.

That was in Toronto or Vancouver. She never said anything about Nathan. Not surprising, considering what happened before I left home."

"Ah ... well, we all have *issues,* don't we?"

"Look, I don't want to ruin this evening for us or the kids." He inclined his head towards Devon and Tyler, still racing cars in the corner of the yard. He came around the table and looked directly into Mel's eyes. "My *issue* with Nathan can wait for another time. It was messy. Enough said?"

She blinked and nodded sharply. Tears welled in her eyes. He put his hands on her shoulders and drew her into a loose embrace. She held herself stiffly but hung onto his arms.

He spoke into her shoulder. "Look ... I'm okay with Edie's anger. I'm not so thick that I don't see what's happening. I'm pretty angry about *my* life too. And now Devon's mad at me and ..."

"Devon's mad?"

"... and I'm certain you have anger *issues* too." He drew back and cocked his head to work a smile out of her with the word issues.

She relaxed against him then raised her head. Their faces were inches apart. He could feel her breathe.

"What's Devon mad at?" She realized she'd overstepped, pulled back a bit. "Oh, sorry. None of my business."

Joe shrugged. "About the same thing as Edie. More disappointed in me than angry." He shrugged again. "He just found out Nathan's alive. Wanted to know why he'd never been brought to see him."

"He and Edie should get along fine." Their eyes studied each other for a moment, drawn to some familiarity in the other, seamed by childhood histories and calamitous events. Each had taken a divisive stance and each struggled with negotiating the rocky journey that is filial duty.

He was still holding her. Her body had loosened under

his touch. The softness of her against his chest was balm to his bruised psyche and soothed the unexpected ache in his chest. He thumbed the tears from beneath her eyes. She ran her hands down the length of his arms and let go.

"Well — you think anyone can eat now?" she asked.

"Beer's great for digestion," he smiled.

☙

Deli cartons littered the table. Devon and Tyler had carried dirty dishes to the kitchen and had disappeared into the living room. Edie joined them for dinner, uttered a ubiquitous sorry, occupied a chair for the remainder of the meal and said nothing. If she'd been a child she would have been called pouty. Attempts to draw her into a happier frame of mind failed. Even when Devon and Tyler provided a mini-theatre with a potato becoming potato salad she managed to suppress a smile.

In spite of Edie's sullen behaviour, Mel and Joe kept up a steady stream of conversation. Mel remembered a community service club festival in the park. Joe said he used to go to them too. He liked throwing balls that dunked the guy into the pool. Did Mel ever play baseball in that empty field behind the feed lot? Sure, she said, it was as far away from parents as kids could get.

But swimming at the lake was the best. The shock of diving into the water on a hot day; the quiet coolness of submersion when all the world was green and floating. The powerful self-confidence in kicking off from shore and pushing the lake behind you until the shoreline stretched like a loosened tether in the distance.

Mel and Joe each sought the memory in the twilit sky. Edie didn't disturb their reverie, taking some of the peace into herself and holding it.

Joe roused first. "Those big parties that Scott's parents threw in the summer. Do you remember those?"

"Oh, yeah. They were made to create memories." She turned to Edie. "Do you remember those, Mum? A bathtub full of ice and cold pop. Imagine the thrill of endless pop when you're nine years old. Charcoalled hotdogs and sloppy ice cream. Could any kid ask for more? It was great."

"Yeah," Edie said, moved to acknowledge a pleasant time, "it was great."

"I just wish I could do that for Dev," Joe said. "Not the same thing in Toronto."

"Do you have to live in Toronto?" Mel asked.

"Well, that's where Dev is right now. And my job."

"Devon's what? Fourteen? It won't be long till he'll be able to go anywhere he likes," Mel suggested.

"Yeah, well, it's a dream, isn't it?" Joe shifted in his chair. Mel watched him tap his index fingers together, musing on the dream.

"Some dreams come true," she said.

The screen door slammed and Tyler rushed into the yard. He grabbed Mel's arm.

"Dad's here," he announced, tense with expectation. "Maybe he brought Spider-man." He alternately squeezed and released his grip on Mel's arm. Mel stilled his hand in hers and stood up.

"Let's go talk to him, then," Mel said in measured tones.

Dono hovered in the front doorway, eyeing Devon who was sitting on the floor in the living room, playing cards spread over the coffee table.

Dono watched Mel approach and flipped a finger at Devon. "You're not letting some kid babysit, are you?"

"That's Devon," Tyler chirped. "We're playing poker."

"What is this?" Dono growled. He turned on Mel. "You're teaching him to gamble, now?"

"I ... they're just playing," Mel said. "Devon's a friend."

Devon came to the door. "Hi, I'm Devon." He put out his hand. Dono looked at it, then at the skinny kid's bright face.

"Don't teach my son to play poker," he said. "Who taught you to gamble?"

"I taught him," Joe said, attracted to the hallway by the Devon's voice. Edie followed behind him. Joe eyed Dono, sizing up Mel's problem.

"Yeah," said Devon, "so we can play Rummoli. I want Ty to learn how to play."

Dono looked at Joe, whose muscled body and greater height dwarfed Dono's slim frame. "Who are you?"

"None of your business, Dono." Mel's voice had the hard edge of protectiveness, an overt challenge to any remaining influence Dono might have on her life.

"It's my business if he's a bad influence on my son." Dono's eyes turned on Mel were defiant.

"You're a fine one to talk." Edie nudged in beside Mel. "You gamble all the time. On people's stupidity, on people's fear, on misplaced loyalty."

"You stay out of this, Edie." Dono's mouth spit out the words, small bullets of anger.

"Mum!" Mel said, worried about retaliation in nasty ways.

Joe stepped forward in a protective stance. He was inches from Dono's face.

"You're not playing nice, Dono." His mouth was tight and his voice threatening. Dono stepped back. Tyler broke the tension of the moment.

"Dad, did you bring Spider-man?" Tyler danced back and forth on the balls of his feet. He wanted to escape the tension in the hallway but not without his superhero.

"Yeah. It's in the car." Tyler darted between them and went to retrieve his precious toy.

They all stood in silence for a moment, taking stock of the standoff.

"Well," said Joe, "I've wondered why Mel lives in a less than ideal situation. Now I know."

"You don't know nothing," Dono snarled, "and you can stay out of my family's business."

"Actually, we weren't properly introduced. I'm Joe Bennett." He paused. "Nathan Bennett's son."

Dono's face turned ashen, his eyes darting from Mel to Joe and back again.

"So, Mel's family business overlaps mine. See how that works?" Joe's confidence in relating this news had the intended effect. Dono floundered for the upper hand and missed.

"I hear your old man's crazy," he said. "And stay out of my business or you'll be sorry."

"I sometimes wish sorry was on my radar, but it's not."

Tyler was back with Spider-man in his hand. "Thanks for bringing this, Dad."

"Yeah, sure," Dono said. Recognizing that he couldn't win this time, he turned and quickly left.

Tyler retreated to the living room. Devon stood in mute shock, flicking the piercing ring in his brow.

"Is everything okay, Dad?" Devon asked." His guileless face sought earnestly for reassurance.

Mel sputtered, "Oh, Dev."

"We'll talk about it, Dev. Mel has enough to deal with." He motioned Devon away in the manner of all adults conveying that the conversation was closed.

Devon joined Tyler and the three adults returned to the back yard. The convivial mood of earlier was gone.

"I guess it didn't help, us being here." Joe offered.

Mel shrugged. "It doesn't take much to upset Dono."

"I think he's getting scared," Edie said, knowingly. "He sure lost his colour when he heard who Joe is."

"He might feel like we're ganging up on him …," Joe said.

"Dono is threatened in many ways …"

"… and take it out on you," Joe said. "Maybe it's time to look deeper," he added.

"What do you mean?" Edie and Mel said in unison.

"Who's the only person besides Dono who knows anything to talk about? Not Nathan." He looked at Edie. "But Owen knows what happened."

"He's always denied everything. Why should he stir up a mess? He's got nothing to gain," Mel said.

"He hasn't got much to lose either," Joe said.

"What are you proposing, Joe?" Mel tightened inside, waiting for the suggestion that she visit her father.

"I could go see him." He looked at both women whose mouths had dropped open.

"Why not? He can say whatever he wants or keep quiet."

"I don't know," Edie said anxiously.

Mel looked at her mother. "You've always wanted to implicate Dono, make him take some of the responsibility. What can it hurt?"

Edie stood up. "Everything," she said and went into the house.

Tyler's excited voice traveled into the back yard. "I got a flush! Isn't this a flush, Dev?"

Devon said way to go and they giggled at Tyler's success.

Mel and Joe sat quietly, wondering if they wanted everything to change.

· Chapter 10 ·

Mel couldn't be hung over. They hadn't even finished one bottle of wine. The grittiness of her eyes told her that it was lack of sleep rather than alcohol to blame for her thick head. It felt like she had dreamed all night. She had been standing on the diving board over a swimming pool about to dive in. Tyler, Devon and Joe were standing in the pool in only four inches of water. They were calling to her. Joe was saying *I'll catch you, you won't get hurt.* She'd awakened with a thudding heart and relief at her close call. She'd padded to the bathroom for some water, then, tossed and turned for hours, disturbed by the dream's risk-taking implications.

Mel unwound the sheets from her legs and dragged herself to the bathroom. She could hear Tyler in the kitchen explaining to his grandmother what the different poker hands meant. That was the good part to remember about last night. Tyler happy and enthused about a friend.

Nice friend, too. Devon was good to a younger kid, played with him at his level then found a way to make them both happy with cards. And the father of the friend was nice too. Nice enough to take a leap into dangerous waters? Does nice cut it or does it take more than that? What would she be leaping into? She thought there had to be some faith in a good outcome to *whatever* she started with Joe. Whatever? That sounded like she was considering something beyond getting facts to nail Dono.

Last evening had set them up as friends, at least. They'd had a great time, had some good laughs, some good memories, and time spent encircled by his arms. It had felt awfully good, leaning on his chest, feeling the strength in his arms supporting her, like giving up a struggle and letting him shoulder it for a while. What is it they say? A trouble shared is a trouble halved. Something like that.

Mel stood under the shower, letting the water pound and soothe her tired body as her mind continued to drift to Joe. He was an unexpected element in her life. She thought she had every reason to hate the Bennetts, but Joe's non-involvement with his family exempted him from that. He didn't have anything to do with his father's complicity, not with leaving town at seventeen and never coming back.

On the other hand, did Joe ever help the situation? She didn't know what she expected. Maybe he should have whisked his mother away and cloaked her with a protective blanket of ignorance. Is Joe's ignorance of events an acceptable excuse for negligence? What about denial? There's a lot more culpability with denial. That seems more like a choice rather than state of being. Joe knew there were felony charges against his father and still didn't come home. That's not really ignorance. But it was a choice that she could relate to. She didn't want anything to do with *her* father's criminal life either.

It was such a mess. Now Joe thinks he should talk to Owen. She's not sure she wants to hear anything from that quarter. Is that ignorance or denial?

Why was she thinking these things? Her head didn't feel like tackling large issues. Life was about priorities. Just find some coffee and get Edie to the bus station.

In the kitchen, Spider-man was climbing the cupboards and rescuing people stranded on a mountain.

"You're safe now, Ma'am," Spider-man told the invisible woman. "I'll go back for your dog." Spider-man made his way up the cupboard again.

"Tyler," Mel said, "have you had enough breakfast? We're going to leave soon."

"He's fine, Mel," Edie said. "He had Cheerios and juice."

"Take the banana, Ty. We'll stop for groceries on the way home. We're going to the lake, to Scott's." Mel felt her mother turn, saw her questioning look. "I'll come back in to pick you up. Don't worry."

When they piled into the car and Mel switched on the ignition, the engine didn't turn over. She tried again. It was dead. Mel hit the steering wheel with her hand. "Damn! Damn! What timing!"

Edie scrambled out of the car. "I'll call a cab and you can call a garage for a boost. I'll still get to the bus on time." She was into the house leaving a dispirited duo behind in the car.

"Guess that's it for the moment, Ty. We'll get there but not for a while."

Edie was gone and a half hour later the garage tow truck pulled up as close to Mel's car as possible. The mechanic lifted the hood of Mel's car to attach jumper cables and stopped still. "Lady, you don't have a dead battery." Mel, sitting on the step, stood up to go and look. "You don't have *any* battery," he said.

Mel stared at the empty space where even she knew a battery was supposed to be. Her mouth opened and closed.

"I don't understand." She looked at the mechanic as if he could explain the missing car part.

"I don't understand," she said again.

"If you don't know where it's gone, then somebody stole it," he said.

"Stole it?"

"Well — what else?"

"I ... don't know. I guess that's it."

"You should call the police, let them know. If you want, I'll go to the shop and bring back a battery."

Mel nodded. "Sure, okay."

Mel made the call to the police who took their time getting to her house. The mechanic had installed the battery and was leaving as the police arrived. He told them what he knew and left.

"You hear anything last night, Ma'am?"

'No. No, I didn't. We were in the back yard, then, went to bed."

"Well, you're not the first person this has happened to. Is your car always parked here, in the driveway?"

"Yeah. Front of the house. There's no place else for it."

"Do have any idea who might do this? Anybody bothering you lately or anything?"

Mel hadn't thought beyond the theft. But now her heart thudded. Maybe ... Dono. Just a little intimidation to slow up the search for the truth? Dono telling her he's still in control of her life? She clasped her hands together to stop them trembling. She didn't want the officer to see her distress.

"I guess it could have been anybody passing by. It's sitting right there, so available," she offered.

"Yeah. That's about the size of it. Of course, your insurance might cover it, depending on your deductible."

"Not likely." Mel grimaced. Another expense. Just what she needed. Dono had probably thought about how that would inconvenience her, too.

The officer closed his notebook. "There's not much chance of finding it. Sorry. If you can give us more information, or remember something ...."

"Thank you, Officer." Mel stood from her seat on the steps. Her legs were starting to shake. "Thanks for coming." The officer nodded and left.

She sat again. She was weak and shaken, vulnerable, like that day in the parking lot. This time he came too close, right into her private space. What if he keeps up the pressure? What if I can't handle it?

Maybe she should take off with Tyler. Get away where Dono couldn't find them. How could Dono find her if she was out of province? She had transportable skills. She could get a job somewhere else. But, however far she went, she knew Dono would come after her. You can run but you can't hide? She had to be stronger, for Tyler's sake. She guessed all single mothers had their fears. Some financial, some feared failure on their own. A few, like her, feared for their physical safety. There was a lot to fear.

In the past Dono had hurt her physically and now he was getting good at psychological abuse. And here she was collapsing under the pressure. What was happening to her? Just a week ago she was ready to fight Dono for Tyler's safety. She'd been angry and strong, a mother tiger protecting her cub. Where did that iron will go? She folded into her lap and lay there to gain strength. Finally, she felt calm enough to go inside and be with Tyler. She couldn't let him see her terrified and weak.

Thank God Edie was gone. She would have gone on a tirade about Dono. She feared that sometime Edie would mouth off in big way and then none of them would be safe.

ಌ

"But, Gram, you *can* go with us," Devon said. "You can go in the back way. There's just one step. Then you walk right out on the deck from inside." He looked to Joe for confirmation. Joe was nodding.

Devon was trying to convince Vera to go with them to Scott's cottage. Vera wasn't jumping at the idea. Joe thought she wanted to go; he could see uncertainty, maybe even some fear, holding her back. She had trouble looking at them, just fiddled with her dress and shrugged I-don't-know.

"If you can't manage the one step we'll just boost you up and you'll be over it with no problem." Devon grinned at this solution. Vera acknowledged that vision with an upturn of her mouth. She reached with a tissue and patted drool.

She gestured to the food stains on her dress. "I can't ... eat away."

"Gram, you eat here," Devon pointed out.

"Dev, I think she's a bit embarrassed about eating in front of others," Joe said softly. He looked at Vera. "Is that it, Mom?"

Vera gave a curt nod and lowered her eyes as they filled with tears.

"Dad, we can fix this some how, can't we?" He took Vera's hand and held it. Devon waited for Joe to make things right.

"Look, Mom. Nobody's going to care how you eat. But maybe we can keep a wet cloth beside you and Dev and I can be right there on either side of you, handing you things and so on." He waited a beat to see if this was making an impression. "There'll be hamburgers and we can cut it up on your plate. And we have to take something, anyway, so why don't we take something you can eat." Vera looked at Joe's face, as if searching for any traces of distaste for this plan, for the honesty of his feelings. Joe's expression registered sincerity in the way he met her eyes. That Joe was less awkward about her debilities was beginning to show. "What about mac and cheese? You used to make the best mac and cheese. Could you show Devon how to make it? I'd love to taste that again."

Devon leaned towards his grandmother, eyes bright and hopeful. "Oh, yeah, Gram. That'd be so great. Teach me. Then I'm not stuck with that orange death in a box that my dad burns. The real stuff. Can we do that?"

"Sheecret's in the mustard," Vera said.

Devon beamed delight.

Joe did a quick grocery run for the three cheeses and mustard Vera asked for. Vera sat at the kitchen table giving Devon instructions while Joe sipped on a beer and watched his son with increasing admiration. Devon worked with the flourish and style of a television-cook-show host and ended with a sweeping bow.

"Uh … um," Vera looked at her T-shirt, blotched with breakfast and lunch. She patted her chest while her eyes searched Joe's face.

"I need … to change," she said. She lifted the edge of the shirt. "Have undershirt."

"We can help, Gram," Devon offered. The look he gave Joe was earnest, expectant.

Joe hesitated. He could disappoint Devon again, right now. Show himself to be the coward he felt he was. He nodded curtly. "Okay."

They trailed into the dining room/bedroom, Vera stumping in the lead. Joe's mind recorded the boxes of incontinent products, the grab bar by the bed, the commode for night time use. Creams and ointments, cotton swabs and hygienic wipes littered the side table. Joe thought he was holding his breath so he let it go.

"You got lots of stuff, Gram," Devon said. If Devon noticed the astringent odour of a cleanser that almost masked the smell of bodily functions, he didn't mention it. Joe was all too aware of it.

Vera took a clean blouse from the dresser and held it up.

"That should be easy, Gram." Devon stepped forward and took the blouse from her. He turned towards Joe, the blouse dangling in his hand, and offered it to his father. Joe moved to take it; he felt the tug of anxiety and the movement was slow. Heat coloured his face and he fumbled the blouse with embarrassment.

Vera worked her good arm out of the shirt and over her head. She directed Devon to put her weak arm into the new sleeve first, then, turned to Joe for buttoning. Vera's breasts lay flat and low under her cotton camisole. He stopped breathing again. His fingers felt like lumps of clay as he worked his way down the front of the blouse. By the time he finished his hands were shaking. When Vera looked up there was moisture collecting in the corners of her eyes.

Devon praised her bravery at letting them do such important stuff.

Joe stood silently, the sharp sting of inadequacy hitting him in his gut. Devon accepted his grandmother with an unselfconscious ease, no apparent anguish about what she can't do, no expectations of her, just eager anticipation for her to enjoy this day, this evening at the lake. All week, he had watched Devon envelop Vera in welcoming arms, having fun with her at the level of her ability. He never pre-judged her. Devon didn't find it necessary to know what to do or not do. It was about acceptance. Could it be that simple?

It seemed to work.

 ❧

Joe, seated beside Vera, watched from the deck as Neil and Marco crawled along the fir tree that was hanging at a ninety degree angle over the water. They each had saws and were trimming branches as they went. Jeremy, Richie, Devon and Tyler stood on the shore, bouncing with anticipation of the "jumping tree" they were about to inaugurate. When the trunk was fairly clean, the boys got into the water to collect the fallen branches and clear the way for launching themselves off this natural diving board.

"Remember, you guys, you have to go at least half way out to have deep enough water. Wait a minute. Jeremy? Come in and get some spray paint. I want you to mark the safe zone," Scott said.

"Good call, Scott," Joe said.

"Yeah, well, they'll have so much fun with it but you have to mitigate the risks a bit."

"I think my mother's having a good time, too," Joe observed. Vera was situated on the shady side of the deck, watching the boys intently. Occasionally, Devon waved at her and she returned the gesture and smiled. Coming in through the back of the cottage had proven easy. With a little boost from Devon she had negotiated the step and had settled into a comfortable chair on the deck.

"She's amazing," Scott said. "I remember her so much younger and energetic. But, she seems to be enjoying herself."

"That's what amazes me. I don't think I could be that content in her position," Joe said.

"Well, we haven't been there, have we? We don't know how we'll handle it," Scott said. "She can still relate to what's happening. Maybe that's what counts."

"As opposed to my father who doesn't know day from night," Joe said.

"Yeah, and you have to wonder if that's okay, too. How much do we want to know about the end of our lives?"

Joe shrugged. He didn't want to think too deeply. Getting his mother here was enough effort for one day. But that hadn't been nearly as difficult as he'd imagined. After he'd buttoned her blouse and his hands had stopped shaking, he had to admit that helping her in that personal way wasn't so bad. It was almost like helping your child who was just as dependent on your capabilities. She hadn't seemed embarrassed, either. She was used to having help. He was the one who had to adjust. More so than Devon. For Devon, issues were black and white. Grandma needs help. Help Grandma.

"We're going to let the paint dry, Dad." Jeremy brought the paint can to the cottage. "We're going to see if we can find tadpoles in the ditch at the back."

Neil and Elaine joined the group on the deck. Neil opened a beer, began talking to Vera and soon had her nodding and smiling. Marion and Elaine carried salads to the outdoor tables.

"Mel should be here soon?" Marion asked.

"Yeah. Anytime. The bus got in at least half an hour ago," Scott said. "I wonder where Marco and Gina are?"

Mel and Edie appeared around the corner. "The bus has arrived," Mel announced.

"Okay, we made it." Marco swept up the stairs carrying a pie. Gina came behind also with a pie. Two young girls followed Gina.

Marco introduced his daughters to Devon. Jenna at sixteen had a long ponytail, sun-streaked and shining. Devon couldn't take his eyes off her. When Jenna sat beside him, her warm tanned leg brushed Devon's. He blushed and took a great interest in his feet. Angela was a nine-year-old pixie in pink shorts and tank-top. She asked where Richie was and took off to the back of the cottage to find the others and hunt tadpoles.

Over dinner, Joe watched his mother visit with the others. She remembered Neil and Marco, knew the families that their wives came from. Elaine told her about the sailing trip she and Neil were planning. Vera let her know about Joe and Devon taking a sailing lesson. It was pleasant — nobody minded the saliva on her chin. When her speech couldn't be understood they were patient. Vera even visited with Edie. Edie was more reticent about a friendly exchange. She seemed to need the example of the others before her self-imposed barriers came down. There was a time in their younger years when the two women had socialized, when Owen and Nathan were good friends, those times when Joe had been there, too, with the younger Amelia. In the end, Edie was pleasant. At least she didn't seem to attach any blame to Vera. Perhaps she was being considerate of Vera's circumstances. Everyone else was doing that. Vera smiled a lot. Joe noticed that. His mother was having a good time.

He was having a good time too. He admitted to himself that he loved this place. Loved the sun sparkling on the lake, the scent of pitch from the evergreens, the sense of life slowed down in a way that could recharge his batteries. He compared it to Toronto, to the soul-crushing pace of Highway 401, to the concrete and echoing noise. Karen had done him a big favour by sending Devon out here.

He watched birds swooping over the lake. A kingfisher dove for his dinner and came up lucky. The air hummed softly with insect life. Tyler was excitedly telling Mel how tadpoles turned into frogs. The kids had put one in a glass jar and Tyler pointed out the budding frog form. This was a good place for kids.

Scott nudged him. "You're awfully quiet there, Joe. Ready for another beer?"

"No, I think I'll just have coffee." He slouched lower into the chair. "Do you ever think about living here permanently?"

"You mean, insulate this and add on to make a real house?"

"Yeah, like that."

"We've talked about it over the years but decided we wanted it to be a get-away summer place. That works for us for now. With the kids this age and the nature of my work."

"You're lucky. From Toronto you have to drive for two or three hours to get to cottage country. Here, you can have it in half an hour."

"Some people even commute to Vancouver," Scott said. "They have jobs that they don't have to go to every day. Business people who can work partly from home."

Lucky people, Joe thought.

The air was cooling as the sun went behind trees and rock outcroppings. Shadows lengthened into inky pockets along the shoreline. Mel got sweaters for herself and Edie. Mosquitoes buzzed their search for dinner. Devon took Vera indoors to play Rummoli with the kids.

After Vera went inside, Mel sat down beside Joe. What does that mean, he wondered? He was alert to feelings tonight. Maybe that came from being more personal with his mother. The closer you get, the closer you feel? He saw her more clearly now. He was starting to see the person underneath the debilitated body. And Mel — there were moments last night when he could imagine he was more than comforting her. The closer you get, the closer you feel?

He sighed.

"The battery was stolen from my car." It was a quiet statement, as if it wouldn't mean as much if she didn't proclaim it.

"What?" Joe swiveled around to face her.

"This morning there was no battery in the car," Mel said.

Edie leaned forward. "You mean it wasn't just dead?"

"No. When the mechanic came and opened the hood, it was missing."

"What's that all about?" Scott asked.

"I had to report it to the police," Mel continued. "The mechanic wanted me to. Then they asked if I have any idea about who might take it. Was I having any problems with anyone?"

"Dono," Joe and Scott said in unison.

"I guess so," Mel said quietly.

They were quiet for a moment, absorbing this new piece of news, considering its implications.

"Christ, Mel, don't take anything from Dono," Marco said.

"Report your suspicions," added Elaine. "Have you done that?"

"No, I ... wanted to think about it. They know about the theft but not about Dono as a suspect. There's no way to prove anything."

"I told you he was scared," Edie said. "This is nothing but intimidation and he has to have a reason for that."

"So was that episode in the parking lot," Joe said.

"What episode?" Edie asked.

Mel waved it away. "A while ago," she said.

"I wonder if the police did anything about Allison?" Joe asked.

Edie looked at Joe. "She got off at Abbotsford with me. I wonder if she has family there?"

"Maybe we should call and find out," Joe said. He looked at Mel. "You know her last name?"

"Hopkins. Allison Hopkins."

"When I take Mom and Devon home, I'll leave them and come by your place. I can help do this."

Mel nodded. She crossed her arms around her body, leaned into Joe's shoulder. He felt her need for security, for comfort, felt her willingness to open herself to trust him. He wanted to put his arm around her shoulders, to let her know that she could lean on him. It felt something like a private moment, but maybe only for him, so he slid his arm across the back of the chair and pulled her closer, and let the others watch him comfort her.

❧

Tyler had fallen asleep in the car and now resisted getting undressed. Mel tested his shorts and T-shirt for dryness. The air had cooled enough for light blankets so she tucked him in clothed.

In the kitchen Edie was putting away food and dishes. She stopped with a plate in her hand. "You're starting to fall for that Joe, aren't you?"

Mel turned sharply. "What?"

"I can see the signs. You think it's a good idea to trust him with this?"

"What? Mum, you're outrageous!" Mel came close to Edie, fixing on her face. "First you want to implicate Dono because it's not fair for Dad to take all the blame. Then when Joe wants to talk to Dad to find out more you think that's a bad idea, too much to lose. Now, tonight, you seemed to think talking to Allison to get information would be okay. Now, here you are, questioning that very thing." She put her hands on Edie's shoulders. "I'm trying to do what's best for Tyler and me."

"And what about me?" Edie asked.

"Oh, Mum!" she dropped her hands to her sides, fists clenched and frustration overflowing. She walked the length of the kitchen then whirled on Edie. "I don't know what you want! You're so full of contradictions. You say one thing one time then jump the other direction as soon as someone agrees with you. What do you want? Do you want Dad to look less guilty by Dono going to jail? Do you want to leave everything the way it is and have me suffer Dono's threats? Do you want Tyler in hospital again?"

"But why do you need Joe Bennett?"

"Why do I *need* him? I don't *need* him. But it feels awfully damn good to share the load! Besides, he has a vested interest."

"Yeah, in you. He can't do anything about his father."

"What's wrong with him wanting to know what happened? He sure can't find answers any other way. And, so what if I'm not at odds with him anymore?"

"Yeah, well. You're so emotional about Dono you might just be seeing Joe as a refuge."

"And what if I am? Everybody needs a place they can feel safe and secure." Mel clasped her mother's arms. Her voice quieted. "That's your problem. You've lost your refuge. You don't feel safe anymore."

The door bell rang. Edie shrugged out of Mel's hands and headed through the hall and up the stairs.

Mel let Joe in and they settled in the living room where there was a computer set up in one corner, Mel's real estate course spread out on the side. The piles of books hadn't moved. There were no bookcases and no place to put a bookcase so the books stayed in stacks on the floor.

When they found the Abbotsford directory they felt daunted by the number of possibilities.

"Well," said Joe, "at least with so many Hopkins they may be related and someone will be able to tell us Allison's whereabouts."

"I'll make some tea, or maybe have some wine?" Mel said. "This could take a while." Joe said yes to wine and they were soon making phone calls. Joe hit it lucky on the sixth call.

A man's voice wanted to know who was calling and why.

"We're trying to find her to ask questions about her employer, Donovan Harris," Joe said. "Harris has been making threats against his ex-wife, Amelia Compton, who is sitting right beside me. We want it to stop. The best way to do that is get some incriminating evidence on him that would open him to criminal charges. We think Allison has that evidence."

There was silence on the end of the line that stretched into a minute. Joe raised his eyebrows to Mel, questioningly.

"Is Allison there or could you have her call us? "By this time, Mel had the phone to her ear as well, her head pressed against Joe's.

"I'm her brother, Wayne. She won't say much about Harris or how he treated her but I've seen the bruises. I'd love to leave some bruises on *him*." There was silence again. "Allison's out right now, visiting some cousins. I'll talk to her when she gets back. What's your number?"

Joe and Mel sat back with their wine, pleased with their progress. They wondered how long they would have to wait for Allison's call. Mel didn't begrudge this time alone with Joe.

The wine relaxed the tension around the phone calls but the air between them was charged with expectation. Mel moved to the sofa and Joe followed, sitting close enough that their bodies touched and shared their heat. Joe lifted his arm and draped it around Mel's shoulders, running his fingers in a lazy path up and down her arm. Mel turned her head and looked up at Joe. She rested her hand on his chest, feeling the movement of his breathing. Joe reached with his other hand to her face, caressed her eyes, traced her hair-line with his fingertips and tenderly outlined her mouth.

Mel was ready for his kiss, her hand slipped around his neck and she pulled him to her. The kiss began tenderly, deepened to hunger, full of want and need. Their lips parted, found a new spot, their longing pulling them to each other. Joe's hand found her breast and brushed it lightly. Mel covered his hand with hers and pressed him to her. He explored her other breast and found the bottom of her T-shirt.

Mel guided his hand to her breast, easing aside the lacy bra cup.

"Joe," she said. "Joe …." Mel pulled back a bit.

"Mel, if you don't want to finish this, say so. I think you do as much as I do. We're not kids." His voice was a soft entreaty.

"Yes, yes. Just let me … check, upstairs. I'll be right back."

She returned in a few minutes, carrying pillows and blankets. "There's no phone upstairs. And they're both asleep."

They settled onto the cushioned floor. "The sofa felt too much like high school," Mel said. Joe chuckled and pulled her into his arms. They found the tempo of where they had left off, clothes disappeared, arms and legs wrapped around each other. Fingers and tongues touched and explored, moving with the intensity of parched travelers. When they came together Mel's release flooded her with an electric wash that filled all the empty spaces inside her. She wrapped her legs tightly and pulled Joe deeper, wanting all of him.

They collapsed together, damp and breathing hard. They held each other until their bodies cooled in the night air. Mel pulled the blankets around them and held Joe close.

She started to giggle and she covered her mouth with her hand. Emotion bubbled in her throat and erupted with a sputter. Joe looked at her and grinned.

"I needed that," Mel deadpanned.

Joe exploded with laughter, pushed his head into the pillow to muffle the noise. They held each other and shook until the wave of mirth subsided. Finally, they dozed, shifted position with arms and legs around each other and dozed again. They were wakened by the phone.

"Hello. Who am I talking to? It's Wayne Hopkins."

"It's Mel, Amelia Compton."

"You're Harris's ex?"

"Yeah. Yes, I am. Is Allison there?"

There was a moment's pause. "No, Allison's not here." Another pause. "She was in an accident on the way back. We think her brakes failed on a corner."

Mel gasped. "Is she ... badly hurt?"

"Yes. Head injuries and some broken bones. She's in the intensive care unit in Abbotsford."

Mel reached for Joe, wrapped his arms around her waist. "Can she talk to you? How bad is the head injury?"

"She's not unconscious, which is a good sign. She's pretty disoriented. The doctors say she could be like that for a while. Really, they don't know, but they said she'll come out of it."

"Hold a minute," Mel said. She related the information to Joe who took the phone.

"Look, Wayne. Maybe I'm over-reacting but I don't think so. Have the car checked for tampering. Mel's car was fiddled with today. Someone took the battery. We think it was Harris trying to intimidate her. He's starting to run scared about what people know and might tell. If Allison knows incriminating information, maybe this was no accident."

Joe waited, listened to Wayne and, finally, rang off.

"He said a mechanic was going to look it over, anyway. It was his wife's car and it's always well maintained. And he'll talk to the police."

"Oh, Joe." Mel's dug into his arms. Tears leaked from the corners of her eyes. "If she'd died, that's murder. Right now it's attempted murder." Mel gulped and swallowed hard. Joe held her tight.

"We've got to press the authorities to look deeper. I think we have enough to make them move," Joe said. He looked at his watch. "It's 3:30. Let's have some tea, then, if you're okay, I'd better get home. But tomorrow we'll talk to the police and decide what to do from there."

"Maybe the thing to do is to talk to my father."

"Yeah, that's looking more necessary all the time."

· Chapter 11 ·

The next morning, everyone slept late. Vera was obviously tired. She insisted that the dinner at the lake had been wonderful, but she walked with more difficulty, patted Devon's shoulder rather than engaging him in banter. She rested and dozed on the sofa all morning. When Joe suggested that they take a day off work, Devon's grin widened. Devon could have some time at the Skatepark, and on the way, Joe would stop at Scott's office to see Mel and set up a time to talk to the police.

His own eyes were gritty from lack of sleep. He carried the rest of his body with a satisfied ease, kind of liquid and slow-moving. He couldn't stop thinking about Mel, the two sides of her life. The loving mother, tenderly nurturing and the hungry, sensuous woman. He found himself smiling at odd times.

He reflected on the way their bodies worked together, that joyful laugh after sex, the softness of her skin under his calloused fingers. He should have removed that band-aid on his left thumb. He wondered if it had bothered her.

Then there was Dono, unpredictable, a menacing presence, making Mel tremble with fear. They had to reel him in, somehow.

Devon followed Joe into Mel's office. He looked around the office at pictures of houses for sale while Joe talked to Mel.

LAZY WATER

Joe knew he was smiling again. Mel's sleep-deprived eyes brightened when she saw him. She grinned back. Joe began thinking ridiculous thoughts about angels with golden hair then stopped himself.

"So," Joe said, "we should go talk to the police. Some time today?"

"Yeah," she said slowly. "I can't see any other way to deal with this. I can go at lunch hour. That's 12 o'clock."

"Sounds okay to me. We don't need to make an appointment, I guess. People walk in with complaints all the time."

"Doesn't this look nice, Dad?" Devon said. He was waving a flyer that advertised a house on a lake. "Great picture. I can almost feel the lazy water"

"Lazy water, huh," Joe said. He looked at the picture and agreed that it was lazy water. "Where is this, Mel?"

"That's on Little Bear Lake. Not too far from here. It's a new listing."

"Nice," Joe said. He put the flyer back. "Okay, Dev, we're on our way." He turned back to Mel. "See you at twelve."

At the Skatepark, Joe found a spot to sit against a tree and watched Devon perform. The kid was good. You had to have youthful agility for it, he could see that. No ratchety joints or brittle bones allowed. He watched for an hour then, satisfied that Devon wouldn't mind him leaving, told him he was going to pick up paint, caulking, and wood filler they needed for inside work. Vera had agreed to sell the car and, since Joe and Devon would be around for a while, Joe was going to use that money to continue upgrading the house. He would also stop at a used car lot to talk about the car sale.

Joe finished his business at the car lot. He didn't expect much money for the car but was surprised at the salesperson's estimate. With a low-mileage luxury car in good condition, depreciation doesn't happen as fast. Some day soon he'd bring it in and Mel could meet him there after work.

Distracted by these thoughts, he only noticed the man and woman across the street when her throaty laugh caught his attention. They were leaving the Ambrose Hotel, arms linked and clearly enjoying themselves. The woman pulled the man's head close and kissed him playfully. She rumpled the man's hair with long, shiny fingernails. A silky, lavender dress swirled around bare legs, catching glints off the sun as it moved. Her spiked-heel sandals pitched her body forward, exposing her cleavage at an inviting angle. Joe recognized Elena Crossini.

Thirty years ago young Joe saw Elena come out of that same hotel with another man. Joe was coming from Scott's. A pick-up basketball game finished early when Marco sprained his ankle. Sitting around while Marco iced his injury had lost its charm and they'd helped him home, leaving Joe close enough to home not to backtrack to Scott's. Joe rounded the corner of the gas station and stopped for traffic at the crossing.

The spring twilight cast shadows over a man and woman coming out of the Ambrose Hotel across the street. They were familiar shapes, the woman's long dark hair rippling over her back, her colourful dress swinging with the roll of her hips. The man had square shoulders that stretched into a solid chest; his suit jacket was hooked on his fingers and fell behind his back. This trait of Nathan's could be a characteristic of many men, Joe reasoned.

Joe blinked to clear his vision, hoping to see something different, something more acceptable. But he saw Nathan and Elena, arms around each other, stumbling out of the hotel, smiling and joking, their voices reaching an intoxicated pitch that carried in the still night air to Joe at the corner. Elena's signature laugh rolled around him, his father answering it with a sloppy kiss on her lips.

Anger and humiliation warred inside him. He wanted to run and hide from this public display; he wanted to run after the pair and knock them each senseless. He felt weak and clammy; the traffic light changed to green; he leaned against the light standard and slid to a crouch when his legs wouldn't hold him.

He watched the couple walking away, happily ignorant of him or his distress. He watched his father's hand grip Elena's buttock, squeezing her 'till she playfully smacked his hand.

When his leg muscles began twitching, he stood. Now his breath was coming in rapid gasps. His groin felt tight, became hard and painful. Anger ballooned in his chest and he ran across the road, cars narrowly missing him and honking their fright. He raced along the street, reaching his father and grabbing his shoulder from behind. Joe pulled Nathan around and hit him solidly on the jaw. Nathan's outrage was slow to develop. Elena started screaming and Nathan landed some punches on his attacker.

When Nathan recognized Joe, he shouted in confusion and raised his hands in the air; Joe pummelled his father with the fury of lost innocence behind each blow. Elena pulled at the back of Joe's shirt, screaming and clawing at him. Nathan lay on the sidewalk with his arms crossed over his head, taking Joe's hits until there was no anger left.

Joe's chest heaved and blood flowed from his nose and lips. His fists were red and scraped. Nathan had quieted, lying still, bloody around his face. Elena knelt beside Nathan, shaking and snivelling, wiping blood off his face with her dress. Joe turned and ran.

Joe rubbed his eyes. He noticed a tremor in his hands. After thirty years the memories were graphic and strong. He was shocked and shamed that he'd responded to Elena's blatant sexuality. He'd blocked that memory over the years. It was far easier to condemn his father's lust as a moral failure and to label Elena as wanton, than to consider his own primal reaction.

He went to his car and sat there, exhausted and trying to reconcile the detailed memory with his feelings about his father.

His mind raced with confusion, then, meanings became clear. He could see that he wasn't just outraged for his mother's sake. Part of his fury was at Elena. She had played sexually-provocative games with him many times over the back fence. She'd used him and his raging hormones for the fun of seeing him squirm and knowing that she had the father wound as tight as a piano string, too. She came on to him, over and over again, and never once allowed him to touch her.

The result was that he was furious with his father. And jealous! A soft groan escaped from his lips. He laid his head against the steering wheel. For thirty years he had carried bitter anger in his gut for a father that deserved the beating. Now he shook with the possibility that the beating was provoked by jealousy, not moral outrage. There was no honour in jealousy. It was pitiful, covetous, unrequited possessiveness.

Goddamn jealousy! He hit the steering wheel with the heel of his hand. Shit, shit, shit! His steely rightness had unravelled.

≈

Mel checked her watch one more time, willing Joe to walk through the door and put her insecurity to rest. She nibbled on her cuticles, a lifetime habit she reverted to when stressed. The Comfort Level achieved with a new partner was tested The Day After and gave some indication of the future of the relationship. Right now Mel was nervous. The Day After was like walking on muskeg, soft and yielding with the threat of sinking. She always capitalized aspects of intimate encounters. Capitals gave important events the status they deserved. Joe had been pleasant and considerate earlier this morning, but Devon had been with him and it was a public place. She had experienced a jolt of longing when she saw him. How they would react to each other when they were alone was still unknown.

Sometimes she abbreviated events to initials — like the L.Q. The Laugh Quotient was a subjective measurement of the happiness she derived from sex. She'd figured out early in her adult life that she felt joyous after good sex, and that laughter was hard to suppress when emotions were high. She'd laughed a lot with Joe and was thrilled when he laughed too. She had rarely laughed in bed with Dono. That's how she knew that their marriage wouldn't last. The L.Q. was far too low.

Joe walked through the door twenty minutes late. She could tell by the tight lines around his mouth that he was stressed. The nerves in her stomach danced around, even as he kissed her tenderly.

"I'm sorry I'm late," Joe said. He raked his hair with his fingers. Wisps of hair stood at odd angles. "I ran into some people ... then I had to pick Devon up at the Skatepark and take him home." He looked at his watch. "Do you think we have time, now? Maybe we could just have lunch and go after you're off work?"

Mel looked at her watch, considered the time to get to the police station, do their business and get back here in forty minutes. "It doesn't seem realistic to do it now. Who knows what's happening at the station?"

"There's a Subway just down the block," Joe said. "Let's go there. We can walk. It'll be fast."

Mel had to lengthen her stride to keep up with Joe who seemed to be racing invisible competitors. Once they were seated with their sandwiches, Joe exhaled audibly. It seemed to Mel that he was deflating after being stretched to unreasonable limits.

He scrubbed his face with his hands. "I'm sorry I was late," he repeated.

She nodded, waiting for him to continue. He looked at the sandwich in front of him as if it were a surprise to him.

"Joe ... if there's something else you should be doing ...."

His head jerked up and he looked at her as if finally seeing her.

"No ... there isn't. I'm sorry ..."

"Stop apologizing! That's the third time you've said that. Whatever it is, you're very distracted. Although I don't know how you can be because, for me, the fact that our lives could be in danger is very compelling!"

"Yes, yes. You're right. "I'm sorry. No, no, scratch that. I *am* very distracted. And I should be paying attention to *our* situation. And I *will* pay attention."

"Does your *distraction* have anything to *do* with *our* situation?"

Joe raised his hands in a defensive palms-out gesture. "Don't get up-tight. You're throwing double entendres at me and I can hardly cope with ..."

"Up-tight!" Heads came up from other tables. People looked quickly at the pair then ducked their heads, both drawn to the personal drama and embarrassed by it.

Mel leaned across the table into Joe's space. "Up-tight? I'm damned near ballistic! My ex-husband just tried to kill his girlfriend and may try to kill me and the man I just slept with seems too distracted to help me deal with it!"

Joe reached across to take Mel's hands into his. "Mel — do you ever think you might be wrong about your father?"

"What! He's a convicted felon. I know he's guilty. How can I be wrong about him?" Mel sat tensely upright, momentarily confused about the switch in topic.

"I don't mean about his guilt or innocence. I mean ... do you ever question your decision not to talk to him?"

"Why are you asking this now? We need to talk about Dono and Allison and what we'll tell the police."

"You didn't answer my question. Do you think some times that you should talk to him?"

Mel pulled her hands out of Joe's reach. "I don't understand why you're interested in this now."

"No, maybe now isn't the right time." Joe looked at her for a moment. "I just wonder if maybe we don't have all the facts, about our fathers, I mean."

"What else do I need to know except that he's a criminal who took people's savings?"

"I don't know. But maybe it's better not to take a stand that puts you on the moral high ground. Cause you can be knocked off."

Mel began gathering her purse and stood up. "I don't know where you're coming from, Joe. I think you might have just accused me of being a righteous prick. But I can cut my father out of my life if I want to and if I think it's the right choice for my son's life, too." She stood to leave then spoke to the floor. "Should we go to the police later today or leave it till another time?"

"We can't leave it, not with the possibility of you being in danger," Joe said. "And for the record, I didn't accuse you of anything."

Mel nodded curtly and left Joe with their uneaten sandwiches in front of him.

Back at her office, Mel deflected Scott's curious looks by shifting papers from one spot on her desk to another. Her busy-work accomplished little, except to occupy her hands and serve as a distraction from the disastrous lunch. In another four hours Joe would be here again and she had no idea how to act around him. Her day that had started with a wonderful post-cloital warmth had quickly disintegrated as Joe ignored their new status as lovers and, instead, probed the minefield of filial relationships. Where was his sensitivity, his understanding heart? What happened to their shared intractability about their fathers' place in their lives?

By 5 o'clock, Mel's anger had worn itself out and had left her with a lump in her throat that pushed tears close to the surface.

"Mel?" Scott stood at her elbow. His concerned voice was all it took to start the tears flowing. She grabbed for a tissue and blew her nose.

"I'm okay, really," she said.

"Well, you sure could have fooled me," he said.

Mel used another tissue. "I can't figure out Joe," she said.

"Oh," Scott replied. "Well, you haven't known him very long."

"No, but, I thought we were getting along, connecting, you know. He was going to help me with the police and sorting out Dono."

"Well, that was just yesterday at the cottage, when he said that," Scott offered. "Don't you think he could still do that?"

Mel ignored Scott's question. She dabbed at tears, adjusted her clothing, cleared her throat and sat up straight. "I'm fine now. I'll work it out with Joe. Thanks, Scott."

Joe appeared at the door, nodded at Scott and looked intently at Mel.

"Well," Scott said, "I think I'll head home. You can lock up, Mel." He shrugged his shoulders at Joe and left.

"I called the police and told them we were coming," Joe said.

"Oh good," Mel said. "We can be quick about this."

"C'mon, Mel, cut me some slack. I have issues, too, and they have nothing to do with you, or us."

"You seemed to think differently at lunch. Your issues were the most important things on your mind."

"No they weren't," Joe said. Mel was standing by now. Joe put his hands on her shoulders. "It only came out that way. My confusion about Nathan got in the way for a while. And I really am sorry."

"Let's go talk to the police." Mel had the door keys in her hand and motioned Joe out.

꙰

On the ride from the police station, the space in Joe's car was filled with a silence so thick that Joe couldn't find any way to penetrate the wall. Mel had returned to the stony silence that had accompanied them to the station. Joe had told the story of Dono's probable assault on Allison and Mel had amended her statement about the missing car battery to implicate Dono as a likely suspect. Joe had tried to impress upon the officer taking their statement that Dono's aggressive actions were escalating, that he'd been threatening at Mel's house on Saturday night. The one piece of hope they received from the officer was that the Abbotsford R.C.M.P. were investigating Allison's accident and would file a report once the vehicle had been examined for evidence of tampering.

The R.C.M.P. officer had advised that Mel to get a temporary restraining order against Dono. At least they could arrest him if he violated the order. That was one concrete accomplishment but it wasn't likely to make a lot of difference to the situation.

Joe drove Mel back to her car, pulled between longing and despair. When he parked the car he tried again to get past the barricade of silence.

"Do you think we made an impression?" Joe asked.

Mel leaned her head back on the seat rest. Joe could see moisture collecting in her eyes. He reached to touch her. She didn't move away as he put his arm around her neck and rubbed it gently.

"You're disappointed in me, aren't you?" He waited a beat. "Join the club. I seem to be gathering in people as I go." He sighed.

"Am I wrong or were things good this morning?" Mel asked.

"Yeah," he said, "I was tired but last night was still fresh and good."

"And then what?" Mel said. "You saw me in the daylight and decided there was too much baggage?"

"It's not your baggage, Mel. It's mine."

"I don't understand what is more important than stopping Dono."

He pulled his arm back and scrubbed his head with both hands. "You're right. We have to stop Dono. That has priority.

Anything else that's knifing through my gut has to wait. It's been there 30 years." It was self-pitying and he immediately wished he hadn't said it.

"You don't have a monopoly on suffering! Besides, your own issues didn't seem so desperately compelling last night. You were able to cope with mine, yours and ours."

"And right now I can't." He turned to her in an appeal. "Mel, did you ever do something big that influenced your whole life after that? And then you couldn't undo it?"

"Yes! But that was marrying Dono and that was undoable. And, I'm sure whatever was between us is undoable too." She scrambled out of the car before Joe could stop her. He called to her from the car window but she found her keys and drove away without looking back.

Damn! The steering wheel took another thump. He didn't need this right now. He sat for a while trying to figure out how that conversation had nose-dived so fast. He needed to get himself together. If he didn't he could wreak the same havoc at home as he did with Mel. He knew he blew it big time. He couldn't explain it to Mel right now. Not till he sorted it out for himself.

When Joe got home Devon was on the phone telling someone about his sailing lesson. He mouthed the word Mom and Joe nodded, got a beer from the fridge and sat at the table. The table and floor were slimed with food debris. Vera had eaten but maybe not Devon. Joe felt an unsettling twitch in his legs and had to get up and move around. He found Vera in the living room watching Wheel of Fortune. Joe thought that she appeared less tired than this morning. He was glad someone had had a good day.

He sipped on his beer and wondered how his own life had gone to hell in about eight hours. When he got up this morning he'd been tired but buoyant. He'd felt that he and Mel had found something special with each other. How quickly it dissolved. And he admitted that it had nothing to do with Mel. She just suffered the side effects of his bummed-out day.

For thirty years he had blamed his father for the fight, for causing the estrangement. He didn't deny that Elena had a seductive charm and he could even view her as a predator. He acknowledged that she preyed on Nathan but, at seventeen, hadn't realized the same thing was happening to him.

What a crock of BS! It made no difference. Nathan knew what he was doing. He knew that he was betraying his decent wife and he acted anyway. It was Joe who couldn't control what he did. It was primal, fighting for the female.

Joe snorted in derision. Man — he was reaching deep for that one. What a cop-out. Vera looked over at the sound. He tried to smile. He reached and touched her arm, connecting with goodness. Vera's eyes widened for a second then smiled back.

"Dad." Devon called from the kitchen. "Mom wants to talk to you."

Karen had had a successful trip to Texas but her friend, Chantelle, was still in Halifax.

"Her sister is home now but not able to look after herself," Karen said.

"That's okay," Joe replied. "It's been good with Dev here."

"Really?" Joe heard the skepticism in her voice and couldn't blame her.

"Yeah. He's great with Mom. And because of him I'm seeing more of friends. Not making this a quick trip has been a bonus."

"Oh. Good." She was somewhat convinced.

"Yeah. We haven't finished the house yet. We've stopped rushing it."

"He told me about the sailing lessons. He sounds happy."

"He is, except … I had to tell him about my father. He was pretty upset that he didn't know."

"Of course he was," Karen said. "I never could understand why you handled things that way. He asked me why I didn't tell him myself. I told him it was your issue. It was up to you to handle it however you wanted."

"Yeah, I know but …."

"But nothing. He wants to see him. You need to tell him something about Alzheimer's too. You can't just take him into a dementia unit and not prepare him."

Joe was silent, knowing she was right, not knowing what to do.

"If you're wondering what to do next …"

Joe chuckled. "You still reading my mind?"

"I always could," she said. "Especially when you didn't want me to. Call the care facility and ask them. They can tell you what to do."

"Yeah. That's a good idea."

"Say hello to Nathan for me. We've never met but …"

"It wouldn't matter anyway. He wouldn't know you. He thinks I'm his brother, Will."

"Oh."

"Yeah."

"It really is too late, isn't it?"

"For everything," Joe said.

· Chapter 12 ·

Joe was restless in bed for several hours before he got up and sat on the back porch. He wished he smoked. He could picture himself sitting, looking at the sky, contemplating the big questions in life and tossing butts into the dirt. It was supposed to be soothing, smoking, if you could ignore the rest.

He sat while the moon rose in the sky, a quarter moon with a long sharp edge carved in the night's blackness. He was wearing boxers and a T-shirt and began to feel the late night chill. The days will be cooling, he thought.

Last night at this time he had been wrapped in Mel's arms, drinking in her sweetness. They'd seemed like they were headed in the same direction, each of them sorting through family problems and finding common ground, then finding each other. He wanted to help and protect her from Dono. It would help him understand what had happened with his father. It could all have worked.

But then he had a meltdown. Not without reason, he gave himself that much. It's a long fall from your self-constructed pedestal to primal soup. He couldn't expect to land softly and get up fully put together.

And how was Mel supposed to know what was happening to

him? As far as she was concerned he had come from her bed, full of tender warmth, expressing a willingness to help her by his phone calls and his supportive presence and he had turned into a self-absorbed, confused jerk.

Mel was wonderful. He wanted more of her. He knew he could make things right if she let him try. He could start by talking to Owen. With that resolved, he finally went to bed and slept poorly. He couldn't let go of the heaviness inside him. He thought of Vera's music. Maybe some Debussy would help. Then again, maybe not. He finally slept.

In the morning he placed a call to the Abbotsford Correctional Institution to find out how to visit Owen. They told him he would have to go on an approved visitors list and that Owen and the authorities would decide if he could see Owen. Since Owen's crimes were non-violent they didn't expect there would be a problem.

His second call was to the Lakeview Manor. He talked to a manager who agreed to meet with him and Devon that afternoon. With these difficult meetings to think about, he decided that the morning should be some relaxing activity.

"Hey, Dev." Devon was skateboarding on the sidewalk, the iPod clipped to his belt. "What do you say to some fishing this morning?"

"Yeah, way cool," Devon enthused.

He called Marco's house to ask about the boat and gear. Joe offered to buy their own gear. Marco said no, just use mine. Well, Joe asked, could he come by and get it? Gina said she'd trade vehicles with him so he could have the trailer hitch for the boat. Devon made them some sandwiches and put them in a bag along with some iced tea. When they left, Vera was sitting on the couch doing crossword puzzles.

"Fish for dinner." Devon promised and kissed Vera's cheek.

They picked up the boat and Devon also promised Gina fish

for dinner. They turned east along Chilliwack Road to find a boat ramp to the river. Devon found everything about the activity an adventure, from putting the boat in the water to deciding which lure to use. Joe was grateful that his fishing trip with Marco had refreshed him on the tricky manoeuvres of boat launching.

"Can I run the boat, Dad?"

"Let's get the hang of these rods — I don't want to tangle our lines — then I'll let you have a go."

With Devon steering the boat, Joe found that fishing left a lot of time for thinking. Maybe that wasn't such a good idea, considering that his thoughts were all confusion. He tried to focus on Devon. Every once in a while something would happen, like loosing a lure or having to restart the motor which choked and sputtered. They had time to talk.

"Dev."

"Huh?"

"We need to talk about Grandpa."

"Yeah." He looked up. "When are we going to see him?"

"Well, the thing is, your mom and I think you need to know something about Alzheimer's disease before you see him. It can be pretty disturbing, Dev."

"Why? If it's all going on in his head, won't he look okay? I mean, he won't look gross or anything."

"No, he'll look okay. To you anyway, because you don't know what a big strong man he used to be. He's ... shrunk. Sort of. To me, anyway. He's gotten smaller since I last saw him. I don't know why. I guess because he doesn't eat like he used to."

"Does it make him feel sick or something?"

"I don't think so. But that's a question we can ask. I think it's because he doesn't know what food is anymore. He isn't interested."

"How can he not know what food is? That's weird."

"I really don't know, Dev. All I know is that people with

Alzheimer's lose their memory. They don't know anymore what things are for so they don't pay any attention."

"But he can still visit can't he?"

"Maybe. Maybe not. He doesn't talk much and what he says doesn't make sense."

Devon sat still, thinking about it. "Grandma still visits."

"Yeah. I know. But she has 50 years of marriage and most of her own life history tied up with him. He's an important connection for her." Joe didn't know if he'd said the right things or not. "Dev, I made an appointment for later this afternoon to talk to someone at the care facility. You can ask all kinds of questions. Me too. But I think we need to do this before you visit."

Devon considered this. "Yeah, I guess," he said. "I wish you'd told me about him. I could have seen him before he got sick." It was a soft declaration with no blame attached to it. Devon concentrated on the motor and the fishing line.

Remorse stirred inside Joe. He willed it away. He didn't need any more moral failures piling up for him.

They fished for a couple more hours, rewarded with undersize trout that had Devon jumping with excitement until they had to throw it back and some lost lures. "That's the great thing about fishing," Joe said. "It teaches patience."

"I don't think that's what it teaches."

"So what do you think?"

"I think it teaches that fish are smarter than we are. We're the ones sitting here in the sun not getting anywhere. The fish are having a good day."

"But I like just being out here. No phones or cars or … or troubles. Just you and nature, relaxing, or trying to." Joe looked at the other boats and the noisy picnickers on shore. He saw a pre-teen drop paper waste in the water. The mother cuffed him across the head. The boy grabbed at it and picked it up. One dog, leashed and tied to a chair, was barking incessantly. Joe took in the noises and thought this wasn't the way to fish. It should be tranquil, like sailing.

"You'd probably like that lake with the lazy water."

"I probably would." Joe looked around. Kids continued shouting at each other and parents acted as referees.

"I wonder where that lake is," Joe said.

"We could ask someone." Devon said.

"Well, we aren't having a lot of luck here. Let's eat our sandwiches and then take a drive."

They stopped at a gas station and asked directions to Little Bear Lake. They were directed back to Sardis and, since they would be passing Marco's place, Joe decided to take the boat to Marco's before travelling the gravel road. As they pulled into the yard Marco and Gina's oldest daughter, Jenna, was picking cherries from a tree in their yard. Each time she reached up, her cropped T-shirt rode high revealing a golden flat stomach sporting a navel ring that glittered in the sun. Her long hair was scrunched through the hole in a baseball cap and fell in a thick ponytail.

"Hi, Jenna," Joe called.

Jenna waved back. Waved to Devon. "Hi, Dev. Any luck fishing?" Devon blushed and waved back, shook his head.

Joe nudged Devon. "Want to go talk to her while I thank Gina and get our car?"

Devon looked stricken, nodded okay. Joe took pity on him. "Offer to help pick cherries and tell her that we're going looking for Little Bear Lake." Devon nodded.

When Joe returned, Jenna and Devon were eating the cherries as they picked. Small piles of pits were accumulating beside them. Jenna was telling Devon stories about the camp she went to. "There was one of those zip-lines, a cable slide, where they harness you in and then you slide along a cable into the water. Wow! It was fantastic. I wanted to go again this year but you can't.

It's so popular you can only go once and then if you want, you can go back as a camp worker. I'm going to do that next year."

"Where's that, Jenna?' Joe asked.

"It's Camp Malibu, at the head of Jarvis Inlet. But hey, Joe, I told Devon I can show you where Little Bear Lake is. If I can come with you, that is."

"I wouldn't mind a guide. How about you, Dev?"

Devon nodded. His mouth worked but nothing came out.

"Go ask your mother. We'll wait for you." Jenna ran into the house and Joe looked at his son. ""Did I do okay by saying yes?"

Devon found his voice and high-fived Joe. "Yes!"

Jenna kept up a steady stream of chatter during the ride. "I was babysitting this morning for Mrs. Granger. She has two kids, Derek and Emma. They're seven and five. She works three days a week so I babysit until noon then their grandmother comes over. During school time they just have after school care."

Jenna sat beside Joe in front and gave directions. "Little Bear Lake doesn't have much on it. There's a campground that kids use for parties because there's only a dirt road and not much traffic."

"If there's a campground, is there a boat launch?" Joe asked.

"Yeah, I think so, but I don't know anyone who uses it. There's the turnoff now," Jenna pointed to the right.

About a kilometre down the road was a For Sale sign pointing right. Joe followed two signs and turned into a lane that stopped behind a large white house.

"Is this the house we saw at Scott's office?" Devon said.

"I think it is. Look at the dormer windows. This is the one." They got out of the car and walked around to the front of the house. It looked empty. "I'll just knock to be sure no one's around." Joe went to the door. Nobody answered his knock. "I guess we can look around."

"It's so big," Devon said, eyeing the house. "Neat, though, eh?"

Joe studied the house. "I can't tell how old it is with this design. It's been well kept."

"But look at the lake. Just like we could skate on it. Lazy, huh?" Devon said to Joe.

"It sure looks still." They wandered through long grass and pushed aside shrubs and flattened blackberry vines to make their way to the lake. The terrain sloped to the lake in front of the house.

"Looks like it was groomed at some time but not lately," Joe said. He peered at the house. "For Sale but nobody lives here. I wonder who it belongs to. Jenna, any idea?"

"Nope. Not me. But my dad or Scott would. That's Scott's sign."

"I wonder if the lake's good for swimming," Joe asked of no one in particular.

"Too bad we didn't bring suits," Devon said.

"Who needs suits," Jenna declared and made her way to the shore and tested the water temperature with a bare foot. "It's soupy," she said. "C'mon, Dev." Jenna plunged in with her clothes. Devon whooped and followed. The kids were swimming, hard, away from shore, shouting at Joe to join them. He stood there, amazed at what was happening.

"C'mon in, Dad."

He took only seconds to take off his watch, his shoes and socks, remove his wallet from his pocket and plunge into the lazy water.

౭

Mel was taking her time tidying her desk. Scott had gone for the day, taking extra hours off before the weather changed. Edie would have dinner ready when she got home. Tonight was a movie night for her and their neighbour, Gert. Mel wanted a quiet night, needed one. She wanted her life back, preferably one that didn't include Dono. She didn't know how to get that, except to talk to her father. There was always the possibility that Allison would be okay and willing to talk. That would depend on how scared she was. It might even depend on how much she could remember after a brain injury. Mel would call Allison's brother, Wayne, tonight.

If she kept focussed on Dono, Allison, her father, she wouldn't be thinking about Joe. That's what she wanted—not to think about Joe. She wondered how she had figured him so wrong. She thought he cared about her, wanted to help. He made every indication that he did, but his own problems got in the way. She had too many of her own, ones that had some urgency to them, to set them aside and help *him* instead of the other way around.

And she'd thought they had something more than a one-nighter, that there were genuine feelings between them. You had to be grateful when you found that. It was rare. She'd kept men at a distance every since her separation from Dono. She was too frightened of relationships and it wasn't good for kids, either, to get attached to some one and then, one day, he was gone. She thought of men passing through her life as serial uncles and didn't want that for Ty. She'd let Joe get close to her, to Tyler. Let him into her heart and mind.

It would be hard to wipe him out. She could still feel the good laughter from last night, could feel Joe's large hands skimming over her body, lingering at all the sensitive spots, causing her to arch and pull him close. Those few hours in her living room last night had been wonderful. The sex, the fun, some one to lean on for the necessary phone calls. So much stress had been lifted by a second person on her side. Her ever-lasting arguments with Edie made her feel like she was totally alone in her viewpoint and the strain of it kept growing. Every fight with Edie seemed like the endless pursuit of the dog's tail as it ran in circles trying to grab on to itself.

LAZY WATER

The briny aroma of clams mixed with lemon and garlic floated in the air when she opened her door. It was reminiscent of The Fish Bowl, a local restaurant they went to for special occasions. Mel lifted the lid off the skillet and inhaled. Edie knew this was a favourite of hers. Linguini bubbled in a pot on the back burner. Did that mean that arguments were put away for tonight? Some kind of truce, maybe?

Last night they hadn't talked when Mel came home from work. Edie was in a pout and Mel didn't try to cajole her out of it. She had just come from the police station, from her argument with Joe, so tired, half destroyed by disappointment and anger, and she didn't care if Edie ever talked to her again. They'd each stayed in their corners and nursed their private grievances. Mel started up her computer and opened her real estate course. The distraction didn't prove strong enough and she spent most of her time brooding. Edie stuck to the living room, put a DVD on and watched An Affair to Remember, crying as she always did at the ending.

Tyler was not happy. He threw Spider-man across the room in contagious irritability and both Mel and Edie yelled at him. Everybody had gone to bed mad.

This dinner could be a peace offering.

"Mum? Ty? Anybody here?"

"Outside," Edie called.

"Everything smells terrific in the kitchen," Mel started.

"Yeah, well, I thought it was time to have something besides deli." Edie said.

"You're right. I'm so ready for real food," Mel said. She sat in a lawn chair and stretched full length, crossing her ankles. "Where's Ty?"

"Upstairs."

"How has today been?"

"Fine."

"What did you and Ty do?"

"We went to the park. Ty played on the climbing things. You know." Then Edie averted her eyes, taking great interest in the ant hill beside the flagstone patio. She looked back at Mel, her mouth set in a straight line. "This afternoon we went to see Vera Bennett."

Mel shot upright. "You what?"

"So what's wrong with that? We were friends years ago. When I saw her at Scott's on Sunday I remembered that we used to visit and talk." As if that was all the explanation needed. "So I went to see her. She needs company."

Mel sat back in her chair, willing herself to relax. She attempted a quiet air of disinterest and didn't look at Edie. "So, what did you find to talk about?"

Edie was silent a moment. "Well, Ty was hurt that Devon wasn't there — we talked about what a nice kid he is and she said he's much like Joe — so he sulked until he went outside with his remote car. You know," Edie looked right at Mel, "she's amazing for someone in her position. You wouldn't expect her to be able to get her thoughts around big topics." Edie sipped her wine.

"I'm getting a glass of wine," Mel said. In the kitchen she rested against the counter, visualizing Vera thinking big thoughts. She wondered where this was heading. She stirred the linguini and the clam sauce. She needed to eat soon. She had baseball at 7 o'clock.

"I need to eat soon, Mum. Baseball," Mel said, back outside.

"Sure, Me too. I've got a movie with Gert." Edie sipped her wine. "You remember she was a church-goer? Vera, I mean." Edie continued. Mel nodded. "We talked about loyalty, marriage, forgiveness." Edie looked intently at her wine. "It was a wide-ranging conversation."

Mel stood up. "Good," she said. She went inside. "Ty!. Dinner."

Mel said the clam sauce had just the right piquancy, enough lemon with a hint of cayenne. Edie said the linguini was good, not great; it had cooked a bit long. Tyler said it was mushy, like fishy oatmeal. He didn't like it. He kicked back in his chair, his hands trapped in his armpits. "I don't want it," he said. Mel could see the intransigence in his mouth and determined arms. She didn't have the energy for it.

"That's fine, Ty. Bed time snack after my baseball game."

"Do I have to go?" he whined.

"Grandma is going out, too, so, yes you have to go with me."

"Will Devon be there?" There was a brief flicker of hope in his eyes.

"I don't know. You can take your soccer ball. There'll be someone to play with."

"Well, I'm going to take my remote car in case Dev is there." His folded arms tightened around him.

"Take whatever you like, Ty," Mel said wearily. She pushed linguini around her plate. Piquant flavour only carried mush so far.

The door bell rang. Tyler shot out of his chair to answer it.

"Mom," he shouted from the door. "Mom, someone to see you."

Edie followed Mel along the hall. Two R.C.M.P. officers stood at the door. Tyler eyed the guns on their hips and slipped his hand into Mel's when she reached him.

"Ma'am, are you Amelia Compton?"

"Yes. What's happening?" She felt Tyler squeeze her hand.

The officers introduced themselves. "May we come in and talk to you for a few minutes?" The older officer with grayed hair at his temples did the talking. A younger version of him, military straight, Kevlar vest over his shirt, stood by his side and nodded and smiled the same message.

"What ... what's this about, Officer?"

"May we come in Ma'am? It won't take long."

"Sure, I guess. Come in."

Seated in the living room, Mel waited for bad news. It was bound to be bad news. "What's this about?" she said.

The older officer continued as the speaker. "We're looking for Donovan Harris. We want to speak to him and we understand you are his ex-wife, is that right?"

"Yes, we're divorced." Mel's stomach heaved, her hands began shaking. She raised her hand to interrupt the officer. "Mum, would you take Tyler outside, out back for a few minutes?" She looked at the officers. "Can I just do this, just a minute, okay?" They nodded. Tyler balked at leaving with Edie. Mel could see Edie's reluctance to leave too. "Mum!" she said with urgency. Edie took Tyler's hand and left.

"Now—what's this about?"

"Yesterday you got a temporary restraining order against Donovan Harris. You claim that he's been threatening in his manner and that you suspect him of stealing your car battery. Is this correct?"

Mel nodded.

"Two nights ago, on Sunday, there was an accident in Abbotsford. A young woman was driving a car when her brakes failed. She was seriously injured and is still in hospital. An inspection of the car revealed that the brakes had been tampered with. Her brother tells us that you talked to him and suspect that Harris could be responsible for this. Is that true?"

"Yes, it's true." Mel's insides were dancing.

"Why do you think it was Harris?"

Mel swallowed hard. "The woman who was hurt, Allison Hopkins, used to be Donovan's secretary and girlfriend. She recently left him. I think from some things she said to me that she knows something about Dono's business that implicates him in criminal activities." The officers nodded encouragement to continue. "She said that she couldn't deal with the files anymore.

Dono had hit her. She had injuries, had been to the hospital." She paused a beat. "She was running away from him."

"And you think Harris has the knowledge of cars to cut the brake lines?" the older officer asked.

"Yes, I think so. He used to fool around with cars early in our marriage." Mel was gripping her hands together.

"You also told authorities that Harris was probably implicated in a fraudulent action that your father is now in prison for?"

"I ... I have always believed he was part of the fraud, but I have no proof." She gathered her thoughts. "Recently he's been intimidating and threatening. I believe he thinks I know something and will talk. We're on very bad terms, as you can tell, and he thinks I'll say something. Because of my father, I guess."

"Can you tell us anything?"

"No! I don't know anything. But he doesn't seem to believe that." Tears welled and Mel gulped hard.

"Ms. Compton, do you believe Harris could have cut brake lines on Ms. Hopkins' car? Is he capable of murder?"

Mel wiped her eyes with her shirt. "I ... think maybe ... yes. He pretended to pull a gun on me, making comments about knowing what's good for me. He ... was violent towards me in our marriage. That's why I left." Mel blew her nose in the hem of her shirt. "Sorry ... it's the tension, I guess."

"Have you any idea where Harris might be?"

"I only know his apartment and office. Maybe if Allison can talk she'll know other places to look."

"If he contacts you, would you call us?" They offered her a business card with phone numbers on it. "I know there's a restraining order but that doesn't necessarily mean he won't try to see you or phone." Mel nodded. The officers left. Edie came around the corner.

"He tried to kill Allison!" Edie said. She waved her arms in choppy motions; her eyes darted around, charged and edgy.

"It looks that way," said Mel. She mopped her face and regained her composure. She looked at Edie's excitement. "This isn't anything to be gleeful about," she said.

"I'm not gleeful. What a horrid thing to say." Edie turned away, "But I hope they nail him!"

※

When they finally came out of the water, they'd lain on the grass and let the sun dry their clothes. Insects buzzed around them. Joe showed them how to whistle with the wide flat grass growing at the edge of the property. Jenna had mastered it quickly. Devon was laughing too much to get his mouth in position to make a sound. Then, there was a frenzied squeaking noise from the grass. When Devon and Jenna parted the grass they found a snake with a mouse half in, half out of its mouth. The head end was squeaking. Jenna shrieked and pulled behind Devon. Devon just smiled at Jenna's warm touch and played the role of brave saviour of young womanhood.

Everyone's spirits were high when they left the property. Jenna said her mother would freak when she saw her, think she'd been in an accident or something. Her mother was always thinking the worst was going to happen, she said. Devon kept repeating awesome, awesome at the thrill of the escapade. Joe just drove the car but noticed his shoulders were less tense.

Devon was no longer tongue-tied in front of Jenna and had chattered non-stop on the way back. "See you, Jenna," he called as she ran into her house. "Yeah, Dev. Whenever you want to swim," she laughed.

Joe pulled into the driveway at Vera's house. "We can change clothes pretty fast and still make that meeting at the care facility."

"Wait 'till Gram sees us," Devon said, running ahead of Joe.

"Gram, Gram! Wait'll I tell you what we did."

The house was silent except for the television, a commercial appealing to constipated viewers promising relief with Metamucil. In the living room they saw Vera's afghan crumpled on the floor. Devon called out, "Gram, where are you?"

They went down the hallway to the kitchen. Vera lay on the floor, her quad cane overturned, her lower clothes wet and smelling of urine.

"Gram!" Devon shouted.

Joe knelt beside her. Her colour was dusky and her breathing noisy. A large amount of saliva had pooled beneath her cheek. Joe went to the phone and placed a call to 911. Then his former military training kicked in. He told Devon to get a pillow and Devon, agitated and scared, rushed to do it. Joe had turned her on her side and they put the pillow under her head.

Devon was choking back tears. "Dad, is she going to be alright?" He looked at Joe with a mixture of hope and fear.

"We hope so, Dev. But right now I can't say." He brushed back Vera's hair. "Why don't you hold her hand, talk to her, let her know you're here?"

The ambulance seemed to take a week instead of ten minutes to get there. One paramedic put an oxygen mask on Vera and checked her eyes with a flash light while a second one took her blood pressure. They bundled her into the ambulance and were gone within minutes.

The ambulance seemed to move far too slowly and Joe had difficulty holding back on the accelerator as he followed behind. If he concentrated on the ambulance and not on who was inside it he could keep a measure of control. Beside him, Devon sniffed and wiped his face.

In the emergency room Joe gave personal details to an intake worker then Joe and Devon were directed to sit in the waiting area. Vera had been taken to an examination room. They watched professionals move in and out of the small cubicle, carrying equipment and calling instructions to each other.

Joe sat beside Devon, his arm around his son's shoulders. Every few minutes Devon stood and paced the room. Joe saw the distress in his son. Devon repeatedly worked his brow piercing. Flick, flick, flick. Joe's own insides were cramping; he felt nauseated and once went into the bathroom but couldn't throw-up. Finally a nurse told them a doctor would come and talk to them.

An Asian man in green scrubs approached Joe. "Are you Vera Bennett's relatives?"

Joe stood up. "Yes. I'm her son, Joe. How is she? What's happening?"

"I'm Doctor Wong. She's still unconscious. She's had a stroke. A major one. She hasn't been responsive at all since she came in."

"Does that mean she won't wake up?" Joe asked. He felt Devon beside him, gripping his arm.

"It's not good but she might regain consciousness. We're going to admit her and monitor her. The next few days will tell us a lot. Right now we've got an intravenous going and oxygen. The most we can do is be supportive." He saw the stricken looks on the two men and his voice softened. "You can go in and see her. Talk to her too. She might be hearing and we don't know it. We'll transfer her soon to the third floor. Oh, the bandage on her left hand is because it's quite swollen. We don't know if she fractured something in her fall. We'll x-ray later."

Joe and Devon were moving towards the cubicle when the doctor stopped them. "If you could go home and bring in the meds she's on that would help. But go see her first."

Joe and Devon approached the bed cautiously, as if any noise would disturb Vera. Her face was pale and sunken under the oxygen tubing in her nose which hissed its life support. Devon was weeping and wiped his eyes and face with the back of his hand. Joe embraced him sideways and hung on.

"She hardly looks like she's there," Devon said. Joe gulped at the reality of the statement.

"Mom," Joe softly touched her face. He ran his hand over her hair. "Mom, we're here," he said. Vera didn't move. Her chest rose and fell in shallow breaths, her lips no longer blue. A face cloth was tucked under her chin and was damp with saliva.

"At least her colour's better," Joe offered. It was something positive to say. He continued to stroke his mother's cheek. Vera's small, wounded body shouted "protect me" and Joe felt an instinctive pull to guard her in her vulnerability. But all he felt was helpless. "Let's go get the things the doctor wants. She'll be settled in a real bed when we come back. That okay?" Joe could feel Devon's hesitancy, distress written in the wet streaking on his face. Devon needed time to gain some emotional distance. Joe had no idea what to do after that.

Devon nodded and patted Vera's hand. His voice was watery. "I'll see you later, Gram."

· Chapter 13 ·

While the coffee pot dripped the next morning, Joe called the hospital and was told that Vera's condition was unchanged. She was still unconscious. Joe replaced the phone and took a deep breath. What a difference twelve hours makes. Yesterday he thought the worst that could happen was that he'd beat himself up over the recollection of the fight with his father. Or maybe the worst would be that Mel would never talk to him again. Those issues had receded to the back burner. The priority was to phone Sandra and let her know about their mother's stroke. He didn't have the mental energy to figure the time difference but he thought it would be the next day in Melbourne so placed the call.

Sandra's phone rang until the answering machine picked up. He left a cryptic message that their mother had had another stroke and was in hospital. Could she call when she got home?

Just as he hung up the phone there was a cheery knock and call from the doorway. Janet, the Home Support Aide was making her way down the hallway.

"Oh, 'morning, Joe. You beat me to the kitchen. Vera stirring yet?"

Joe had totally forgotten about the morning help and at that point suddenly remembered that they had missed their appointment at Nathan's care facility too.

"Janet, I'm so sorry. I didn't think to call anybody."

Janet stopped her prep activities and glanced at Joe. "Call anybody?"

"Yeah. Not good news. My mother's in the hospital. She had a stroke yesterday." He thought for a minute. "I wonder what happened to the help last evening. We were at the hospital till after ten."

"A stroke! Oh, no. The poor dear. Is she going to be alright?"

"This morning they say she's still unconscious." His voice dipped. "It doesn't look good."

Janet's eyes teared and she dabbed at them with her finger. "I'm so sorry." She turned. "May I use your phone? I'll just call the agency and let them know to cancel service for now."

Joe nodded and stepped aside. Janet left quickly with wishes for Vera's recovery.

Devon was finally stirring upstairs. They'd left the hospital around 10 o'clock last night when they were both exhausted. Earlier, they'd eaten in the hospital cafeteria, a short refuge from the hectic sounds of clattering machinery and of distraught patients calling out for attention. Joe wondered how anyone got well in the chaotic atmosphere of the hospital ward.

In the hospital cafeteria they'd eaten dry sandwiches which provided fuel for their bodies but were sadly lacking in culinary inspiration. They'd made feeble jokes about patients making fast recoveries in self-defense. Joe had been glad to see Devon smile. The grim situation had knocked him sideways for a few hours. But now that the shock was wearing away, Devon was at least coping.

Joe had gained some balance too. He shouldn't have been surprised about the stroke. He'd been well aware of Vera's frailty ever since he'd got home, but over time had seen the inner person that was still whole. Well, the inner person can function all it likes, but if the body decides to throw a clot, there's nothing about playing crib or doing crosswords that is going to stop that happening.

They needed a good breakfast, comfort food, sticky with syrup and heavy with carbs, food that brings a few contented moments at the start of the day. He would make pancakes. Finding no pancake mix he settled for French toast. There was no bacon — he guessed Vera couldn't chew bacon — so the eggy toast oozing with maple syrup would have to do.

Devon came into the kitchen, his face pale and sleepy, his hair still wet from the shower. The blond spikes lay flat against his head, bony angles giving him the look of chronic undernourishment. Joe added another slice of bread to the egg mixture.

"Did you call the hospital?" Devon searched his father's face for signs that meant good news.

"Yeah. I called. She's just the same."

Joe offered orange juice. "I'm making French toast. Okay?"

"Sure, sounds fine," Devon said without enthusiasm. He sat at the table and stared out the back doorway. "It'll be hot at the hospital," he said.

"Yeah, probably. Later."

Silence settled around them. They ate the French toast, each absorbed in his own thoughts. Joe allowed himself to drift between sadness and lost hope. He heard the kitchen clock ticking in the stillness. He thought it was ticking off the time left in Vera's life. The quiet and the sweetly satisfying food relaxed him, lulled his ragged emotions. It wasn't a bad place to start the day.

"I called my sister this morning. Sandra? She wasn't home but I left a message."

Devon looked up. "Should I call Mom? She'd want to know, wouldn't she?"

"Yes, of course. She'd want to know." Joe looked at his watch, knowing that Karen would be in her office. "Yeah. Call her at work. She'd want to know." Joe regarded Devon, saw the dispirited slump of his body. "Would you rather I did it?"

"No. I can tell her."

Devon made the call while Joe cleaned the kitchen. They had to go to the hospital but Joe didn't want to stay there all day, more or less on a death watch. It wasn't good for Devon either. The hospital would be the first stop then he'd think of something else, something to ease the tension and let their minds focus on less depressing things.

Devon said Karen wanted to speak to him.

"Yeah, hi, Karen. Yeah, not good." Joe listened to his ex-wife for a minute, momentarily satisfied with the sincerity of her concern. "Okay, yeah, I'll ask him and see. Do want to talk to him again?" Joe passed the phone to Devon. "She wants to know how you feel about staying here?"

"You mean, like, go home instead?" Devon took the phone. "No, Mom, no. I'm staying. Gram is sick and I've got to be here." He waited while his mother talked. "Yeah, sure. I'll call tomorrow." He hung up.

Devon looked questioningly at Joe. "I want to be here. I can, can't I?"

"Sure, Dev, sure. Gram'll want to see you when she wakes up."

The phone sprang to life startling them. Joe grabbed it and talked briefly with the Abbotsford Correctional Institution. Owen Compton had agreed to see him and it had been okay-ed by the authorities. He could visit any day between two and four in the afternoon.

Joe had totally forgotten this piece of business. At the moment he couldn't think what he wanted to say to the man. He knew it would help Mel and that was important but he would have to wait for a clearer mind to deal with it.

༄

"I can tell you're upset. Something happened." Scott stood facing Mel's desk, arms firmly crossed and with a serious tone that meant to get at Mel's problem. "You can't sit there looking like the fox being chased by hounds and not expect me to ask … and expect an answer." His voice softened. "Mel, are you alright?"

Tears welled and Mel cursed the weak grasp she had on her emotions. She grabbed a tissue. "Why do you have to be so damn nice?" She blew her nose. "Why can't you ignore my feelings like your friend, Joe?"

Scott raised his brows in question. What did Joe have to do with this?

"I see how you're looking," Mel said. "I don't want to talk about it. Okay?" Mel tidied her face and composed herself behind the desk, sat straight and tense and started opening mail. She worked at ignoring Scott's presence.

"Is that it?" Scott asked. "Is Joe the problem? If it is, that's your personal business, but if it's Dono, or something else I can help with …."

Mel's rigidity evaporated. She didn't have the strength to maintain it and she slumped in the chair. Scott would help her carry the burden of Dono, at least. The possibility of Dono attempting to murder Allison took this problem far beyond the chaotic emotions that made up her life right now.

"The police came to the house last night."

Scott's mouth opened and closed. He pulled a chair close to Mel. "What's going on?" he said.

"You know Allison, Dono's girlfriend?"

Scott nodded. "She's his office assistant too, right?"

"You know she left him?"

"Yeah, you said that the other day. Is this about her?"

"Yeah. She went to her brother's place in Abbotsford. Two days ago she was using her sister-in-law's car and the brakes failed. She ended up in hospital with a head injury, broken arm and bruises."

Mel took a breath. "They checked the car for tampering." Mel took another breath and swallowed hard. "The brakes were tampered with. We think Dono did it."

"Wow. Man, Dono's gone way beyond angry. This is desperate. They really think that Dono would do that?"

"Who else? Dono's the one with something to lose by Allison not toeing the line. If she has turned against him enough to leave her job, and has taken secrets with her, Dono may want to silence her."

"What did the police want from you?"

"Just did I know where they might find him for questioning and did I think he was capable of doing that." She paused. "And maybe to let me know that he was dangerous and I should let them know if he comes around."

"Do *you* think he's capable?"

Mel looked at Scott. "I got a restraining order against him the other day. I think he stole my car battery. Just an intimidation to make me scared."

Scott moved close and took her hand. "He tried to scare you a while ago too, in a parking lot. Pretending he had a gun."

Mel pulled back and released her hand. "How do you know about that? I didn't even tell Mum."

Scott hesitated.

"Oh, I know. Joe told you."

"Quite a while ago, when he'd just arrived. He mentioned it just after you were at our cottage one time." Scott was thoughtful. "Mel, do you think you're safe, I mean at your house? Should you move somewhere else till this is over?"

"Well, I …." She stopped and sat there, moving that thought around, considering the implications. How could she possibly handle Dono if he came to her house? She had nothing but a piece of paper that said he couldn't be there. Big help that was! Nobody paid any attention to a restraining order if they didn't want to.

"I need to think about it. Where would I go? There just isn't any place."

Scott was thoughtful. "You know you're welcome at the cottage anytime but there's no room for anything prolonged." He paused while ideas took shape. "If you came to our house in town, Dono would find you. He's smart enough to think of that." He paused again. "We handle some rental properties. I could find you something. You could just move and he wouldn't know where. Do you want me to look?"

Mel peered at the floor as if the answers would form there, concrete and possible. She couldn't afford two rents. But how much is her life worth, or Tyler's? She'd have to move permanently in order to afford it. Maybe Scott *could* find her a place. Maybe she should just leave. That idea was gaining strength. Dono would never find her in a crowded eastern city. She should just pack a suitcase and disappear.

"Okay. You think about it and so will I." She didn't need to decide today.

The phone rang. Mel had been so deep into confused thinking it startled her. She recognized Joe's voice immediately.

"Hello, Mel." He stopped a moment. Mel sensed he couldn't decide what to say next. She couldn't seem to help him. "I ... need to talk to Scott."

She passed the phone to Scott. "Joe," she said, her tone flat and edged with hurt.

Scott listened "Oh, no. Oh, that's no good. You're at the hospital now?" Mel tensed up. The hospital? Her stomach turned over.

"I'll be right over." Scott hung up. "Vera had a bad stroke yesterday. Joe and Devon are at the hospital now."

"How bad?" Mel asked. She was trembling.

"She's not conscious since it happened. When they got home yesterday afternoon, they found her on the floor." Scott wiped his hand across his eyes and turned away. "I'm going to go see them.

Probably won't stay too long. Think I'll phone Marion first." He went into his office.

Mel covered her face with her hands and groaned. She didn't need to add any more confusion to her churning emotions. She was already cycling between anger and longing and fear and relief at having help from Joe and now …. How long can you stay mad at a man you care about and whose mother is gravely ill?

❧

Joe and Devon had stayed at Vera's bedside for most of the morning. Her condition hadn't changed. Joe thought you could lose her in the large and functional hospital bed, her humanity overshadowed by stainless steel and venous drips. Bed-side rails squealed for oil each time the nurses cared for her, turning, creaming, changing padding that soaked up bodily fluids.

The atmosphere was alien, the impersonal room soul-wrenching. Staff went about their busy-ness in a detached manner, trays and equipment in hand, calling out to other staff for help and to pass information. There was a hard crash in the hallway followed by cursing. Bells rang with unrelieved stridency giving the impression that no one was listening.

Devon's questions broke the tension with a nod to practical matters. Why did they look under the covers like that? Aren't they going to feed her more than water? Why do they keep taking her blood pressure? Joe didn't know the answers.

The attending physician finally arrived, reviewed Vera's chart and spoke to the nurse. He explained to Joe that Vera was critical, that the outlook wasn't hopeful, that she might not wake up. Devon choked back tears and Joe gripped him hard. Joe could barely absorb the staggering events and he couldn't think of anything to ask the doctor that would help him cope. They sat beside Vera and held her unbroken hand.

Suddenly, Scott was standing at the door. "Hi, guys," he said, his voice gentle.

Joe's eyes brightened. "Hi, Scott. Thanks for coming."

Scott gave Devon a hug. "How are you guys doing? Awful question, I guess."

"We can hardly believe it. So sudden," Joe said. Devon was nodding.

"She broke her hand," Devon pointed out.

"Like the stroke wasn't enough," Joe added.

Scott gazed at Vera. "I remember her so active. You know, always baking for someone or organizing a raffle or something." His eyes lingered on Vera's very quiet form. He looked at Joe. "Have you been here long?"

"Not too early, around nine, ten. I don't know."

"Scott looked at his watch. It's about noon now. You want to go grab a snack? I'll stay here a while if you want."

Joe looked a Devon who nodded. "Sure," Devon said.

"We'll be in the cafeteria. I think it's basement level."

"Don't rush. I don't need to be anywhere for a while," Scott said.

Joe and Devon had a mostly silent meal. Joe was finding it hard enough to adjust to this crisis, but a quiet Devon was unnatural.

"Dev," Joe said, "This is all very foreign to me and for you too." He took a beat. "Is there anything you want to ask the doctor or the nurses?" He ran his hands over his face, rubbed at his eyes. The strain made him want to wash away tension.

"Do you think she's going to die?" Devon's eyes were moist.

Joe could hardly say what he knew needed saying. He regarded the table for a moment.

"Dad?"

"Dev, the doctor said she might not wake up. It doesn't look good." Joe looked directly at Devon. "I'm glad you came this summer." His voice was thick.

Devon bobbed his head, swallowed. Took a great interest in his Coke and balled up the plastic wrap from his sandwich. He touched the brow piercing and flicked it a couple of times.

"Let's go talk to Scott," Joe said.

Joe heard voices in Vera's room as he rounded the edge of the door. Mel stood by the bed in deep conversation with Scott. Joe inhaled and felt a knot in his stomach loosen. Even with the tension of the hospital room, Mel seemed composed. He watched her smooth the sheet covering Vera and brush strands of hair from her face.

"Hi, Mel," Joe said.

"Hi, Mel," Devon said. Joe's tone was quiet while Devon's held a degree of enthusiasm. Mel turned to their voices.

"Hi," she said. "I'm … so sorry this is happening."

Joe bobbed his head in acknowledgement.

"She broke her hand too," Devon said, indicating Vera's wrapped hand.

"It doesn't seem fair, does it?" Mel said.

"Uh, Joe," Scott said, "Mel's here for a bit so I'll go back and hold the fort at the office." He stood to go.

"Uh, Dev, would you like to come with me and you can spend some time with my boys this afternoon? We've started building the boat."

Devon started to protest but Joe cut him off. "I think it would be good, Dev. I'll come get you later and you can come back." Joe looked at Scott who nodded.

"Sure, Dev. There're a lot of hours in the day," Scott said.

On the way out Scott leaned towards Joe. "At the cottage later?" Joe nodded.

Joe and Mel were standing each side of the bed. The silence thickened and Joe cleared his throat.

"Thanks for coming, Mel."

"Of course I'd come." She looked up at Joe thoughtfully "There was one time at some gathering, I can't remember which one. We were all dressed up so it was a wedding or something. I was five or six. I couldn't be bothered staying inside the hall with grown-ups so I was playing outside." She looked up at Joe. "I fell, slid on the grass and slid into some dog turds."

Joe snorted a laugh. "Sorry." He mimed zippering his mouth.

"Anyway, I was nearly hysterical. My mother had bought me a new dress and shoes and they were pretty messed up." She smiled. "Vera had stepped outside for a cigarette.

"I'd forgotten that she used to smoke," Joe said.

"Yeah, anyway, she was standing on the steps and I was crying and she came over and comforted me. Then she took me into the washroom and cleaned me up." Mel paused, smiled. "It must have been an awful job for her." She touched Vera's hair again. "By the time my mother saw me again, the dress and shoes were clean and dry. She looked directly at Joe. "I was so grateful and I've never forgotten it."

"She helped a lot of people." Joe turned to the window and then back to Mel. "I missed a lot of it I guess."

Mel shrugged. "Choices," she said.

"Yeah," Joe said heavily. "Mel? Can I tell you what made me so upset that day? What made me leave town." He wanted so badly to make things right with Mel.

She looked at Vera. "Would she want to hear it?" she said.

"Maybe she knows. I don't know." He took Mel's arm and moved her towards to door. "They tell me she might be hearing us say stuff."

Outside the room Mel stopped Joe with a hand on his arm.

"Joe ... this isn't the right time."

Joe felt her reluctance. He didn't know where it came from. Was she withdrawing from him altogether? Did she not want his confidences? "Yeah. Yeah. I see that."

"Another time, okay?"

"Yeah, sure."

"I'd better get back to the office." She put the palms of her hands on his chest. Joe gripped them.

"Mel...."

"Another time, okay?"

"Sure."

· Chapter 14 ·

Over the next week Joe and Devon spent mornings and evenings with Vera, both discouraged and resigned when each day she was like the one before. By the end of the week, the doctor was starting to talk about discontinuing the intravenous in favour of a nasal feeding tube. He wanted Joe to consider the pros and cons of this. Alternately, they could just discontinue the I.V. The implication hung heavily in the room. Was there other family Joe should talk to? Would Joe like to talk to a counselling service … or what about the hospital's Pastoral Care?

The thought of this huge decision left Joe winded. He couldn't get his mind around the fact that this doctor was asking him to decide on his mother living or dying. It was too much. He'd talk to Sandra, see how she viewed the big picture. Even though Sandra wasn't coming home, Joe valued the support she offered. The whole thing was a shitty milestone he didn't want to face.

During that week Joe and Devon swam at Scott's cottage in the afternoon. The boat building was progressing slowly but with enthusiasm. Scott had borrowed some power tools and they all tried vainly to follow the directions that came with the boat kit. They struggled with equipment and had to go to the internet and a marine building supply outlet for help. But gradually the boat took shape.

One afternoon, Joe suggested that he and Devon go for another sailing lesson instead of going to Scott's. Devon thought that would be way cool. By now, Joe and Devon took the boat out by themselves. They caught the small breezes and tacked along the shoreline.

Devon lay on the boat deck, giving Joe a turn at the rudder. "Do you think Gram knows we're in the room?" Devon's eyes were closed, the weak breeze tousled his hair and the sun's glare washed out his facial features. Joe couldn't tell by looking if this was a question for information or one with hurt attached.

"What do you think, Dev," Joe said in his best shrink voice. "Do you get any feeling about it?"

"Sometimes. Sometimes I think she's in there, listening. I almost expect her to answer me."

"Yeah?"

"Yeah. Sort of like you do when I talk to you but you're only half listening."

Joe smiled. "Do I do that?"

"Oh, yeah."

"What makes you think I'm not totally hearing you?"

"'Cause you just kind of smile at me, like you haven't heard but don't want to let me know that."

Joe raised his eyebrows. "Maybe I just don't know what to say. Sometimes you astound me."

"Astound, huh." Devon considered this. "Maybe Gram just doesn't know what to say. Maybe, she's astounded at what's happened to her and is just speechless."

Joe smiled. "I think you're right," he said.

A week after Vera's stroke, Joe was getting restless. The doctor had made it clear that if Vera survived she would be in worse condition that before this latest stroke. She would be unable to return home and they would have to look for care facility placement in keeping with her needs. Knowing that his mother would never be home again, Joe asked Devon to help him move Vera's bed back to the upstairs room that had been hers. He relocated the dresser into the bedroom and cleared away all the care supplies. The dining room furniture went back into the dining room. He called the Home Support office to ask what to do about the grab bar and commode. They gave him the address for returning it.

Together, he and Devon stripped the wallpaper from the hallway and dining room. The house would still be for sale no matter what the outcome for Vera. The house looked more like how Joe had remembered it with the dining room restored and the bedrooms intact.

Each day the air was heavy with humidity and the incessant whir of insects that cruised in the stillness. Bees worked the flowers, loading up with pollen which eluded them in windy conditions. One night on the back porch, Joe saw a lightening bug and showed Devon how to catch it in a jar. Devon was fascinated by the cleverness of nature. Devon got out his iPod again, found the batteries dead and bemoaned his lapse at plugging it in to charge.

One day, with Devon at the lake with Marion and the two boys, Joe wandered through the house. He found himself touching things, the china cabinet, the bookcase in the living room. He spent an hour sorting through books his father had collected, regional history books and Joe found them all in the case. A few more had been added since he'd left. One held a Christmas greeting on the flyleaf. Merry Christmas, Dad! Love, Sandra.

Joe tossed it back on the shelf. He was too late, wasn't he? Too late for his mother, his father, for family memories that weren't rooted in righteous anger.

He heard a timid knock at the door. Marika stood on the porch, a plate of muffins in her hands. "Lemon-poppyseed," she said. Joe welcomed her, led her back to the kitchen. She asked how Vera was doing and Joe said, much the same.

The dining room door stood ajar and the changes in the room made Marika gasp, her hand to her mouth.

"Oh, oh, this means she's not coming home, doesn't it?"

"I'm afraid so. She's still not conscious."

Marika sat heavily. "Oh, I'm so sorry. She's been such a good friend and good neighbour."

"I know she relied on your help. I want to thank you for that."

"Oh, that's nothing. She helped me too, back when she could."

"Did you know her for the whole twenty years you've been here?"

"Oh, sure. She came over when we moved in. She was so kind. Then I found out she liked playing crib and that was that. We set a regular crib date for Friday evening. Been doing it for fifteen years now."

"Did you see much of my father?"

"Not much. But they did have parties here sometimes. Your mother liked to do dinner parties. Really fancied it up with her china and crystal. Once she suggested we start a gourmet club and do a traveling dinner once a month. I don't remember, really, how that ended. Except we tended to come here for the main course and we just drifted back to dinners at the Bennett's. Aw, I'm going to miss her."

They were seated at the table and Joe got up to plug the kettle in and to make tea. "You'll have some?" He indicated the tea pot.

"Sure, I will. We'll try my muffins too."

"So — there were a lot of parties here?"

"More than any other couple. Your parents did like company."

"Was Dad the type of guy that helped with prep? Or did my mom do it all?"

"Ah, he helped, in his way. Not with the cooking or like that. But he was so proud of the way Vera laid a table and dressed the room with flowers and always looked so good herself. He'd go shopping with her for clothes, you know, and wanted her to have the best. You could just see how much he cared about her."

"Did she talk about him when he was getting sick?"

"Oh, yes. You've got to talk to someone, you know. It was such a heavy burden for her. And then when the criminal charges were laid … well, she near fell apart for a while."

"What helped her get it together again?"

"Well, the disease was showing itself and she convinced herself he couldn't help it. That he was too mentally unwell to know what he was doing." She shrugged. "Maybe, he was."

"And if he wasn't?"

"Ah, well, she had her faith. Forgiveness. She was, is, a very forgiving person, your mother."

Joe focussed on the wall.

"Once I asked if her kids would be coming for a summer visit, or something like that. She said no, they weren't, but that it was okay 'cause you were just human. Imperfectly human like the rest of us, she said. You won't find perfection except at the side of God, she said."

Joe stared at his feet. "She said that? We were imperfectly human?"

"That's how charitable she always was."

"I guess she's about as close to perfect there is."

"I always thought so."

With Marika gone, thoughts of forgiveness and a charitable heart turned over in his head. He didn't know if he had the capacity to forgive Nathan or himself. Remorse had filled him for the last few days, remorse for his absences, for his deficiencies as a son, as a father, as a husband. How could his mother be good of heart when the people around her were constantly disappointing her? Vera must have a very spiritual core to be able to see the good, forgive the bad and go on loving.

His thoughts wandered to Mel. He hadn't seen her since that day at the hospital. He had felt her longing to repair the riff between them. He wanted that so much. But he felt suspended in a limbo with his mother's situation — nothing happening that was good and no way to change that — every day like the one before. He hadn't agreed to discontinue the intravenous drip. Sandra had said that discontinuing it was the thing to do. He could see where the doctor was being realistic. The doctor could have refused to let Vera die regardless of her prognosis. He should feel less pressure because of that but he didn't. Last night's phone call to Sandra left them both in tears. Coming to terms with their mother's death would take time. Presently, he was a mess.

Mel …. While she might be weakening towards Joe, there was no forgiveness in her for her father. They'd talked at the hospital again but Vera's presence in the room commanded all their attention and all the social exchange each could manage.

He could still go and see Owen, hope for some morsel of information that would help Mel out. Joe didn't have anything to lose and Mel might have something to gain. He needed to be active to shrug off the melancholy he was stuck in.

Joe popped a beer and looked around the kitchen. It still looked much like he remembered it as a child. They had updated the appliances and work surface but not the cupboards. He could paint those or buy new doors. Maybe that was the way to go, get new ones for a more modern look. He'd deliver Nathan's car to the sales lot today, have money to buy supplies and get that out of the way.

He checked the time and decided it was too late today to go to Abbotsford to see Owen. He'd buy paint and look at cupboard doors today, put the car on the lot and feel like he had some control over his life.

The days turned into another week. Joe still hadn't made a decision about Vera nor had he gone to see Owen. He knew Vera was receiving good care and that allowed him to take his time over this irreversible choice. But in the end it was moot. Yesterday, Vera was showing signs of pneumonia. They decided not to treat her and the intravenous line was taken out. Now, it was just a matter of time.

Devon seemed more accepting of his grandmother's situation and told Joe that he could see that this wasn't much of a life for her. He took the CD player to her hospital room so she could listen to the classical music she listened to at bedtime. Devon was sure her eyes twitched when he turned on Mahler's 4th Symphony. But Joe could see that even the crescendos didn't make her stir.

Their progress on the kitchen and dining room facelift made Devon proud. "Gram would like it too," he said. Joe continued to engineer breaks away from the hospital to counterbalance the sadness and tension of Vera's room. With the temperature still hovering in the high 20's and some days pushed to 30 degrees Celsius plus, the prospect of working on the house repairs for any length of time strained their working relationship. Instead of finding relief at beaches and ice cream stands, Joe thought it was time to do something different.

By Thursday, Joe was ready for that break in routine. He called Scott and asked him about the cottage on Little Bear Lake. Would it be alright if he and Devon went out there for a swim? They wouldn't go near the cottage, of course, but if anyone was likely to be around there …. Scott assured him that no one was around. The owners were the children of a couple now deceased and they all lived out of province. Sure, Joe could go there to swim.

"Dev, should we ask Tyler to come with us? And Edie too if she wants to."

"Yeah. That'd be cool. Can we buy some root beer or something to take?"

"Yeah. We can stop for whatever."

Edie answered Joe's call. She agreed that Tyler could go with them. Far better than Ty spending his day with an oldster, she said. Actually, she said, it would give her time to do some work around the place. And maybe even get to the library. She would show Joe how Tyler uses his inhaler. Now he's supposed to use it before exercise. Joe said no problem.

"Lazy water," Devon said. "I remember the lazy water."

"It'll sure be still today. There's not a breeze out there," Joe said.

Tyler was ecstatic about the outing with Joe and Dev. He danced around the porch while Joe and Edie talked about the inhaler. Ty gave a confident "yeah, yeah," when Edie pressed him about indications for the inhaler. He just wanted to get going.

The lake didn't disappoint any of them. Its warmth and silkiness soothed frazzled nerves. Tyler loved that he could walk out to his chest before there was a drop-off. Joe showed them how to skip stones across the water. He made eight hits. Devon managed six. Ty's stone sank at one. After practice he managed two and whooped his glee.

They lay on the grass and let the sun soak into them. Devon and Tyler spotted a whispy, white cloud that looked like a giraffe. Joe thought it was more like a dinosaur. Joe batted at flies and mosquitoes and finally decided they had to leave. They had plans to see Nathan, not that he would understand Vera's collapse, but they had to see him, at least. And Joe hadn't let the facility know about Vera's stroke. He wanted to do that and apologize for missing their meeting last week

When they dropped Tyler at home he said he would only let them go if they promised to pick him up again some day. Edie smiled. They promised.

After a quick change of clothes they were at the care facility. Joe had prepared Devon for the locked doors but no amount of talking could take away his shock on entering the dementia care unit. A long-term care aide was trying to persuade a resident to go into a bathroom with her. The odour of soilage permeated the hallway. Along the corridor, two women were each pulling opposite arms of a sweater stretched between them. Mine, mine came from their mouths. A man seated in a chair by an open doorway was taking off his socks. He explored one with his mouth. A nurse walked past them and towards the struggling women. Joe heard her mutter something about a full moon. Joe put his arm around Devon's shoulder. "This is why we needed to talk to somebody first." Devon nodded, wide-eyed.

As they approached room number twelve, Joe said, "Remember I said he won't know you. Even when we say you're his grandson it won't mean anything. You okay with that?"

Devon nodded. They entered the room. Nathan was standing beside his bed, pulling at the covers. The pillow and pillowcase were separated at his feet on the floor.

Joe said, "Hello, Nathan."

Nathan turned to the voice. Gray stubble dotted his chin and the remains of lunch dotted his shirt. Joe supposed the nurses were too busy today breaking up fights and fishing for socks in people's throats to get around to grooming.

Nathan looked at Devon and a stricken look passed over his face. His arms started flailing. "Help, help me." His shouted in terror until his diminished physicality betrayed him and he collapsed on the bed, his arms crossed protectively around his head. "Don't, don't, don't hit me," he said, his voice low and weak.

Joe and Devon stumbled backwards. "Dad! Dad!" Devon grabbed Joe's arm. "What's he doing? What's wrong?" Tears glistened in Devon's frightened eyes. Joe's heart thumped in his chest.

"Let's go outside, Dev." He pulled Devon's shoulder and guided him out of the room. By this time two nurses were by their side at the doorway.

"What happened? Did he fall? Is he hurt?"

"No ... no, he just started yelling when I spoke to him."

One caregiver, with gentle understanding, gained Nathan's trust and soothed him with assurances of safety. The other turned to Joe and Devon. "He'll be alright. It's a delusion. He doesn't see what we see. It's part of the dementia." She led Joe and Devon to chairs near the nurses' station. "Sit here and recover yourself," she said. "Can I get you some juice or water, maybe?"

Joe hugged Devon to him, then, feeling Devon's need to sit straight and controlled he let him go. "I ... didn't know that could happen," Joe said. "I'm so sorry, Dev." Joe twisted his hands together. Devon worked his piercing. The nurse brought them drinks.

"He'll settle down. The next time you visit he'll probably be totally different."

"We were supposed to talk to someone before I brought Devon to visit. We both need more information. But ... my mother, Vera, Nathan's wife, she had a stroke. She's in the hospital."

"We were wondering why she wasn't in. I'm sorry to hear that. How is she doing?" The nurse leaned towards Joe. She was too close; he could see the pores in her skin and her dark roots sprouting into a brassy cap of hair. He pulled back a few inches.

Joe glanced at Devon. "Not good. She's been unconscious since it happened."

"What happened to him?" Devon asked, inclining his head in the direction of Nathan's room.

"He probably had a delusion. His mind works differently now, doesn't connect to reality as well. And when he does think about things, he's mostly in the past." She waved her hand at the ward in general. "That's why the old pictures on the doors, so the residents can recognize their own rooms. They're old pictures of themselves and they likely see themselves in the past and expect to look like they did decades ago."

The second nurse returned from Nathan's room. Her name tag said Claire and Joe recognized her from his first visit. "He's calm now. I soothed and distracted him and put him in his chair to rest. I left the radio on. He seems to like classical music. By now we all know which station to bring in." She smiled.

"That's like Gram," Devon said.

"Yes," Dark Roots Nurse said. "Vera plays the radio when she's here."

"Do you think I should go back and see him before we leave?" Joe turned his questioning face to Claire.

"Why don't I go with you? Maybe your son, is it Devon? could stay here until we see how settled he is." Claire and Joe stood in Nathan's doorway. Nathan reclined in his La-Z-Boy chair, his eyes closed, Mozart washing over the room. Joe's heart wasn't thumping as hard now.

"Can I just bring Devon here so he can see him quieted down?"

"Certainly. Good idea," Claire said.

Devon viewed his grandfather from the doorway, his brow furrowed, trying to figure out the whole scene. "He seems fine," he whispered.

"Yeah, now he seems fine."

When they got into the car, Joe was glad to see that Devon was calm.

"I'm sorry, Dev. You've had more than enough shocks this trip."

Devon was quiet for a moment. "It couldn't have worked with Grandpa even if he hadn't got upset 'cause he doesn't know me. I would have had to be here years ago for that." He stopped. "But, Gram. I've had Gram."

His son had wisdom that continued to astound him. Devon may have rationalized Nathan's outburst but Joe couldn't do it. With unwelcome insight he was sure Nathan wasn't having a delusion. Nathan had looked at his grandson, saw Joe as he was thirty years ago, and freaked out about being beaten. Joe couldn't rectify anything. It was too late. Devon might hold on to some disappointment with his father, but he wouldn't have the regrets his father had.

༒

Mel caught the fly ball and stumbled backward, finally coming to a hard stop seated on the ground. It was no softer than the last time she did it, about 5 minutes ago. At least the team was winning, if not the in-fielder.

"Way to go, Compton!" The team shouted their enthusiasm. Mel stood and shook herself. She threw the ball to the pitcher and brushed the grass and dirt from her shorts.

"I didn't think I needed to take out insurance just to come to practice," Mel called out. She heard guffaws from her teammates.

"Toughen up, Compton," they yelled back.

Mel took her position again. Her eyes quickly scanned the park area to check on Tyler. She could see him by the bleachers, running away from Angela who was blowing soap bubbles with a wand. They were laughing, tagging each other, Tyler returning the tag with Spider-Man. Tyler stopped and turned on Angela.

"Take that, you alien invaders!" he shouted. Spider-man broke one bubble after another and saved them from the bubble-invaders. Angela chased him again.

The ball action grabbed her attention again. A grounder to the pitcher for an easy third out. She trotted to the infield; they were switching positions and Mel lined up for a turn at bat.

Mel twisted around, checked her clothes for grass stains, and, laughing with the other players, she saw Dono behind the wire fencing, back of the bleachers, motioning Tyler to come to him. Tyler searched out Mel, hesitant, then, walked over to Dono.

201

Mel shot from the batting line, rounded the bleachers and grabbed at Tyler's shoulders. Dono was still on the other side of the wire fence. She pulled Tyler against her; he startled with a loud Oh!

"I'm allowed to talk to my son, Mel. You can't stop me doing it." Dono's tone was belligerent. Mel was glad the fence was between them.

"I can and will stop you seeing him," Mel countered. "I have a court order. You can't come near me which means you can't come near Ty." She felt Tyler squirming against her legs, the angry tones making him agitated.

"I don't think that's the way it goes," Dono sneered. "I have rights. That's a court order too."

"Well," Mel said, "Go ahead and try to enforce it. You might be surprised at how things come out," Mel said, sure in her position. She could feel Tyler's chest moving against her legs. She saw the beginning of distress in the tight in-drawing of his neck. She had to get him out of here.

"You upset him with your threats, and you can be sure he hears them as clearly as I do." For a moment she wondered if someone with a cell phone could get the police here in time to pick up Dono. She looked around. The team was busy with batting and fielding and no one looked in her direction.

She would try to bait him. "If I feel like it, I might let you see him in a park one day." Dono was listening. "I need to know where you are — so I can call you, if I feel like it." She finished lamely. Tyler's breathing was becoming audible.

"It'll be on my terms. I'll call *you*." Dono spun on his heel and walked away.

Mel didn't relax until Tyler used the inhaler and was settled on the grass.

"Okay now, sweetie?"

"He nodded. "I don't want to see him," Tyler said. "He makes me have breathing attacks."

"I can see that, sweetie. I just said he could see you so he'd go away." Mel leaned back against the fence and exhaled noisily.

"Are you having breathing attacks too?" Tyler asked. His small face was raised to hers and worry lines were etched on his brow.

She hugged him. "No, no, not at all. We'll just keep you and Daddy apart for a while. That should help us both."

Tyler nodded, solemnly.

Mel stroked his head. They'd go home soon.

An hour later, Tyler was bathed and in bed. Mel had read a chapter of Lemony Snicket: A Series of Unfortunate Events. They were on the third book in the series and Mel was thrilled when Tyler helped with the reading.

"Way cool. That's what Devon says, way cool."

"You had fun with Devon and Joe today?"

"Oh, yeah! We went to this super place to swim and had root beer and I learned to skip rocks. I got two rings."

"Wow, that's great." Mel had overheard Joe's phone call to Scott. Sounds like Little Bear Lake was a winner. "Nice lake, huh?"

"Yeah. Dev calls it lazy water. I don't get that but he says it's because the water's so still and perfect and warm, like laying in a hammock on a sunny day. That's what he said."

"That really sounds like a winner place. Dev's kind of poetic."

Tyler nodded, thinking about poems.

"Did Devon or Joe talk about Mrs. Bennett? Joe's mother?"

"No. Not much. Dev said they needed a change."

"Yeah, I guess. It would be hard to watch someone so sick." Mel had been in to see Vera twice since the first day. Vera hadn't changed. It seemed to be a wait-and-watch situation.

Tyler nodded again. "I'm glad we're not sick," he said.

"We're just fine, Ty, just fine."

With Tyler in bed and Edie at the movies, Mel sat at her computer. The online course wasn't engaging her mind at all. If she could just get past the book work and into the field of sales she thought she'd be fine. Maybe it was the wrong thing to do. But right now she had no thoughts on what the right thing might be.

Her mind was too scattered. She had to call the police and let them know that Dono was still around. She was very nervous about Dono. She couldn't trust him and she felt like she and Tyler were sitting ducks for his unpredictable behaviour. Whenever he wanted to find them, he could.

With a flash of clarity she realized that she didn't have to flee to find security. All she needed to do was hide. She especially needed to hide Tyler. She shot up from the chair and paced the living room. Scott had been right that she could live somewhere else and Dono wouldn't be able to find them. She could hide in full view but still work. She would have to be sure Dono wasn't following when she left work, but they could be safe. Scott had suggested one of their rentals, but she couldn't afford that.

She paced the kitchen, put the kettle on for herb tea.

The house at Little Bear Lake! With the vendors out of province, no one was in it and no one would be around. She could camp there. Tyler would love it. Scott would be angry if he found out. His integrity as a business man was at stake. But so was her life and Tyler's and possibly Edie's. Dono wouldn't hesitate to attack whoever stood in his way.

She wouldn't let Scott find out. If he showed the property to a buyer she'd deal with it then. Dono's harassment shouldn't go on too long anyway. Something had to give.

· Chapter 15 ·

The next morning at the hospital, Joe found that Vera's condition had marginally worsened. Nurses moistened her lips and mouth frequently. Even with the oxygen prongs in her nose, she looked peaceful, not at all distressed. Peaceful and pale, Joe thought. Devon rubbed her good hand with cream and told her about swimming with Tyler at Little Bear Lake. Joe had to leave the room when his throat choked with a large lump. Scott arrived and took Devon to the cottage with him.

Joe left for Abbotsford around one o'clock. It might take him an hour to find the prison and be just in time for visiting. The security procedure only took minutes as he was searched going in and personals such as watch wallet and keys were stored in a locker to be picked up on exiting.

Joe didn't recognize the bloated and ill-looking Owen Compton when he entered the visitors' centre. His face was the colour of ripe tomatoes and clashed with the orange prison clothes. His eyes were tight slits that hardly admitted light. He stared at Joe through the narrow openings as if trying to place who he was.

"I can see your old man in you," he offered.

"You've changed," Joe said. "It doesn't look like prison agrees with you."

Owen shrugged. "Neither does high blood pressure and kidney failure." There was a wry smile.

Joe nodded, curtly.

"I used to like your mother's cooking. How's she doing?"

"Not well," Joe said.

"I heard that."

Joe looked at him.

"Edie told me last week."

"Thanks for asking about her but I didn't really come for a social visit."

"Maybe we should just forget it then." Owen made a move to get up.

Joe waved him down. The guard watching from the viewing window started towards the room. Joe waved him back.

"Sorry ... Owen ... I'm pretty up-tight. Lots of stuff happening with my mother."

"Yeah, well ...."

"I won't bug you. I just want to ask a few questions."

"For old times sake and all," Owen said, sarcastically.

"Sure. For old times sake." Joe kept his tone even.

A silence stretched between them.

"Look," Joe said, "do you know Mel's in danger?"

Owen's eyes widened as much as they could. "What kind of danger?"

"Dono's been threatening her. He seems to think she'll tell authorities something incriminating. She says she doesn't know anything."

"And ...?"

"We think he cut brake lines on Allison Hopkins car. That's attempted murder. Do you think he'd hesitate to harm Mel if she seemed to be a threat to him?"

"Do you have any proof he did it?"

"No. But we think he also stole her car battery to scare her.

He's a danger, Owen. To your daughter. To your grandson. His whole attitude is threatening whenever he talks to her. She got a restraining order but paper won't stop him if he thinks he has to "deal" with her. You know what I mean? " Joe regarded Owen. Could see his mind working.

"Yeah, I get it."

"Do you have any information that could stop this? Something the police could use?" Joe's voice took on an urgency. "If he's using crystal meth like Mel thinks he is, he'll do anything. You know that."

Owen sat in silence. Joe let him consider the implications of "do anything" and waited.

Owen looked at Joe. "What's your interest in this?"

Joe waited a beat. "Mel." He stopped. "I'm … I want to help Mel. And Tyler. They're wonderful, Owen. You're missing a lot."

"I'll be dead before my sentence is up." He waited a beat. "Do you think she'd visit me?"

Joe let it hang there a moment. "Right now, she says not. But if there was some reason for her to change her opinion of you … who knows."

Owen shrugged. "I don't have anything to lose either way."

"Oh, yes. You have a lot to lose. Family is everything."

"You're one to talk." Owen was sneering. "Leaving Nathan a bloody mess and never coming back."

Joe startled at this. "He told you?"

"Oh, sure." Owen waved his hand at this old news. "I knew about Elena. She was like an obsession with him." His head jerked up. "He loved Vera, you know. Would do anything for her. But he couldn't shake the magnetism, I guess it was, of Elena."

Joe sat there, looking at him. Thinking about the magnetism of Elena.

"Men are strange animals, Joe, hurting their own. Other species do it physically. We do it every possible way you can think of."

Joe waited for more, felt Owen condemning him along with every other male on the planet.

"What do we do next, Owen?" he asked.

"*We* don't do anything." He was bitter, determined. "You look after your family. I'll look after mine." He got up, signaled the guard he was finished and left.

Back at home, Joe sat in a dispirited gloom. He had no idea what, if anything, Owen could do. He didn't even know if Owen's assertion that he would look after his family meant anything at all. Joe was nursing a beer when the phone rang.

"Hey, Joe. It's Marco."

Hi, Marco."

"First, I want to ask how Vera is," Marco said.

"She's poor, Marco. They've stopped treating her." Joe swallowed.

"I'm sorry as hell to hear that, Joe. Anything I can do? How's Devon doing?"

"He's coping. He seemed to get to a realistic acceptance faster than I'm doing."

"Well, that's partly because he doesn't know her well. Also the young are resilient."

"Yeah. Their own mortality doesn't play a part in how they cope. I see it as the end of an era — and we're next."

"I hear the gloom and I don't blame you. I'm calling to invite you to a party. I know the timing might not be appropriate but maybe you need to lighten things a bit."

"What's happening?"

"We always throw a B.C. Day party at our house. The civic holiday's coming up this weekend. The party's Sunday 'cause everyone's off work Monday. It's an all day deal. We start with a fishing derby then eat anything we catch for dinner. If we don't have enough fish we buy B.C. products like chicken or something to barbeque. That's the firm rule. Everything we eat and drink at the party has to be grown in B.C. Not only is it a B.C. holiday but our famous local corn is ready so that's a feature too. Everything else comes from people's gardens. There's always lots of food so don't worry about bringing anything, except maybe beer or wine. That's a B.C. product that's easy to come by."

"Why don't I bring a dozen corn too?" Joe said.

"Sure. Sounds good. Do you and Devon want to come fishing in my boat?"

Joe thought a moment. "I'll go in to the hospital early and as long as it looks okay, Dev and I will go with you."

"Sure," Marco said, "9 o'clock okay at my place?"

"Sure. See you then."

Joe could feel himself lighten at the thought of socializing without a hospital room as background. If he felt that way, Devon must need the break too. The party was coming at a good time.

ಶಿ

Mel took the long way home from work — by way of Little Bear Lake. She'd taken the key from the office and wanted to check out the cottage before committing to a short-term move. Already, she was feeling some sense of relief. Just having a plan was a positive step.

It took twenty minutes to reach the Mortimer place. She was surprised and pleased at the style and beauty of the cottage. Really, it was more like a house. She circled the property on foot and saw no signs of occupation. With the key in the lock she opened onto a country kitchen. A maple harvest table sat in the middle of the room flanked by ladder back chairs. The appliances were white and '50's vintage. She flicked a light switch and found the power off. She could work around that with a portable gas barbeque and buy deli whenever canned soup and hotdogs lost their appeal.

Tyler would love reading by candles or flashlights. They'd wash in the lake and could go to their house if they started smelling too musty.

There was furniture covered in dust sheets. Living room, bedrooms, a flush toilet in a two-piece bathroom. "It's do-able," she said aloud. Outside, she stood on the porch and gazed at the lazy water. Dev has the soul of a poet, she thought.

She started making mental lists of supplies she would need for a few days, maybe a week. She'd bring towels and dish soap, bath soap, blankets and pillows. It might mean two trips. They could relax here for a while. She just had to elude Dono when she was leaving work. If he discovered them missing from the house he'd tail her and they'd be helpless against him. By the time she locked up she had her family firmly housed in the cottage by the lazy water. Toilet Paper! She couldn't forget toilet paper. She whirled on her heel and headed for her car.

"Is this really necessary? I mean, hiding out?" Edie's tone was incredulous. "We can handle ourselves around Dono," she declared.

"Dono nearly killed Allison — on purpose! Yes, we need to hide out! Besides, it's more like camping. That's what we're telling Ty. We're camping at the lake." Mel moved towards her mother. "Mum, I need some distance from this. Dono is unpredictable. Drugs make him unpredictable. You may think you can handle yourself around Dono but I can't and certainly Tyler can't. I've got to protect him." She was packing duffle bags for herself and Tyler. There was a box of cooking supplies ready in the kitchen.

"I'll take you and Ty on the first trip. We need to stop for some candles and gas canisters. Then I'll have the whole car for the second trip."

She moved out of the room gathering towels and blankets as she went. They went into a black garbage bag.

She took Edie's hands in hers. "Please, Mum. Just do this. It won't be for long. Dono either gets arrested or I do, for break and entering. Either way Dono can't get at me." She looked Edie straight in the eye. "You think I'll look good in prison orange?"

"Probably better than your father," she said.

· Chapter 16 ·

By Sunday morning Vera'a breathing was more shallow. She was still peaceful and pale and Joe decided that going fishing was the thing to do. He and Devon would go to the hospital again sometime after the fishing derby and before dinner.

Marco had Angela in the boat with him. "Jenna's with the Grahams," Marco said. "Annie Graham's her best friend and that's four to their boat too." Only Joe knew the disappointment that Devon must be feeling.

Marco offered sunscreen around and ensured that Angela kept her hat on whether she liked it or not. She didn't like it.

They were fishing Little Cultus Lake for brook and rainbow trout. The fish were sleepy early in the morning. Marco kept them entertained singing snatches of arias from Carmen.

"I didn't know you liked opera," Joe said.

"I was brought up on opera," Marco said "I didn't like it back then. Couldn't understand what my folks saw in it. But there were always records around. I usually just left the room when they played them. Now I love it."

"You even have a voice for it," Joe said. Marco shrugged.

A fish hit Devon's line. With excited laughter he brought in a 16-inch rainbow trout.

"That's your supper, Dev," Angela smiled.

"Whooee!" Dev shouted.

The bite was on and Marco got a keeper. Joe's line tugged and he let Angela bring in the undersized fish. Everyone said aah when it was released.

Within another two hours they had three keepers. Marco and Joe were ready to call it quits. "We won't starve," they promised.

"Marco, I think we'll go and change clothes then make a stop at the hospital before we go to your place."

"Okay. See you at home later."

After showers they bought a dozen corn on the cob and Kokanee Beer. Marco had assured Joe that another guest always made home-brewed root beer for the kids for this British Columbia-only party.

At the hospital they stopped at the door to Vera's room. The oxygen hissed quietly. Joe could see that Vera's breathing was shallow and too fast. She looked so small in the sturdy metal bed that Joe could feel his mother disappearing.

"Do you want to talk to her, Dev?" Dev nodded. "You can talk to her later, too, you know. After. We can all do that." He looked at Devon whose eyes welled. Devon understood.

They stayed a couple of hours, creaming Vera's hand and feet. Dev described the fishing derby to her. The fish got bigger in the telling and Joe smiled. They told Vera they'd be back later tonight and tell her all about the B.C. Day party.

When they arrived at Marco and Gina's there were tent awnings in the yard. Jenna stopped them as soon as they got out of the car and sprayed green streaks in their hair. "I'm keeping British Columbia green," she laughed. Devon loved it.

There were coolers of root beer and real beer. Lawn chairs dotted the yard. A volleyball net was stretched between two uprights at the bottom of the garden. Several teens were batting the ball over the net and whooping when they scored. A small black dog with a green stripe down his back barked each time the ball was hit. Younger children had a garden hose running on a plastic lawn slide and splashed down the length of it in glee. Wet green streaks flowed from their hair over their shoulders giving them a ghostly glow in the bright sunshine.

"I can't see Tyler at the slide," Devon said.

Joe tried to pick out Mel. There must be thirty people in the yard.

"Maybe they're not here yet," Joe said. He presumed Mel, Edie and Tyler would be invited. Devon gravitated to the volleyball net and Joe found a chair beside Scott.

"Marion's inside helping Gina with salads. She said they'd bring the corn for us to husk. That's male work," He winked at Joe. "We'll get the kids into it," he said. They sipped their beer and watched volleyball for a few minutes.

"I think she's going to die soon," Joe said pensively. He was stripping the label off the beer bottle with his thumb nail.

Scott looked at him. "How are you holding up?"

"Not too bad. Dev's pretty good too. We can see this isn't the way for her to live. I'm glad for us that she didn't die immediately. It's given us time to adjust to the reality of it. And I can't see that she's suffered. So …."

"If you need us to take Dev for a while just say the word."

"He's been amazing. But thanks," Joe said.

"Dad," Jeremy called from the porch. "Mom wants the fish filleted."

"More men's work," Scott said.

"I'll get Dev and we'll do ours too. I don't think he's ever filleted a fish."

By this time, moose sausage sizzled on the barbeque. Corn was in huge pots on the stove with more piled on the table. Outside, picnic tables were heavy with salads and relishes, bottles of wine and iced tea in pitchers; beer and root beer were buried in cooler chests of ice. Bowls of golden peaches waited for the ice cream dessert.

Kids started lining up with paper plates and teen plates were heaped to the point of buckling. The fish went on last and sent sweet scents of lemon seasoning into the air.

Many of the people at the party were schoolmates of Joe, Scott and Marco, old acquaintances whose faces and waistlines had aged 30 years. Some were new faces too, neighbours of Marco and Gina and more recently moved to the area to escape city living. Joe met Marco's work colleague, Emmett who lived down the street, and who couldn't stop talking about winning the fishing derby with a six pound salmon.

Devon was surrounded by other teens who were recounting fishing stories. Dev told them his fish was the first he'd ever caught. They couldn't believe it was his first and that led to more "first" stories. Everybody's fish was huge and tough to bring in.

Mothers followed small children around with sunscreen in their hands; teenagers sneaked sips of their fathers' beer; dogs barked excitedly as kids shrieked with water guns; some parents turned a deaf ear to cries for fairness in a game.

The party gained volume as food, beer and wine disappeared. By eight o'clock, the adults were betting on their skill with a hula hoop, that they could beat the kids for duration any day.

Occasionally, Joe would look around the yard to see if Mel had appeared. He was puzzled by her absence. Thoughts of Dono and cut brake lines flitted through his mind. He'd leave for the hospital soon and … drive by her house? At least he could see if she was home.

He found Scott and told him he wanted to go to the hospital for a short evening visit. Could Scott look out for Devon? Take him home with him if the party finished before Joe got back?

When Joe drove past Mel's house and saw that no one was there he got a cramp in his stomach and his palms were sweating. It *could* mean she was just out somewhere. Or it could mean something worse. He didn't know what to do so he just continued to the hospital.

As soon as he got to the ward, two nurses stopped him and said they'd been trying to reach him. Could he sit in the lounge with them?

Vera had died. It was quiet and peaceful, they said. She just stopped breathing. She was still in her room. Did he want to see her? Joe nodded, his throat too full to speak.

As Joe looked at his mother's small body in the bed, he didn't think anything about death could be quiet and peaceful. Death could not be subtle. It filled the room with its overwhelming stillness. The sounds of silence reverberated in waves of sadness. He turned on the CD player to cover the noise. Strauss waltzes overtook the quiet. He listened and let the music soothe the ragged edges of his heart. Joe stood by the bed a few minutes. He touched Vera's hand, her face. He left the music playing and turned and left the room.

He couldn't go back to the party, not like this and he would give Devon another few hours of his grandmother. He drove in circles for a while and found himself on the road to Little Bear Lake. It was dark now and the blackness of the rural sky enveloped him. The house stood starkly against the moonlight. He saw a car in the shadows so left his car on the road. He walked to the edge of the property, not wanting to draw attention and lay on the grass. He looked up at the sky with his arms extended cruciform, or as an angel.

The earth had cooled in the night air. He welcomed it into his fevered body. He heard crickets' sounds and rustling in the grass. A raccoon on a nightly prowl? He breathed in the scent of pine and grass and thought about the end of life.

A flashlight beam tracked across the lawn. Mel bent over him. "What are you doing?" she said. "You frightened me. Then I saw your car. How did you find me?" There was a tight edge to her voice. The flashlight threw a halo of light around her face.

Joe sat up, his forearms resting on his jack-knifed knees. Now the night seemed less empty.

"My mother died," he said. "Vera's gone."

Mel gasped. She leaned into him and put her arms around him. "I'm glad you're here," she said.

· Chapter 17 ·

Guests circulated in the house on Sycamore Street, the women in ubiquitous *TAN JAY* and pearls and the men in dark suits and ties. No amount of speculation could rightly guess their ages. Joe and Devon had avoided the ties but had agreed to dress pants and cotton shirts. Joe didn't believe clothes decreed the sincerity of your feelings.

There were about ten people there who knew Joe. There could have been nobody who remembered him. Mel, Tyler and Edie were among the ten. The Reverend Foster was still drinking tea. He had come to the hospital before Vera died so Joe had made his acquaintance before the funeral service.

Devon found a corner of the couch, and was soon pressed into conversation with Marika. Nathan's violin sat on a side table. Marika asked him about the violin. Devon picked it up and laid it across his knees.

"Is it yours now?" Marika asked.

Devon raised his eyesbrows in wonder. "I ... don't know. Maybe."

"Maybe you could learn to play it," Marika said.

"Maybe," Devon said, uncertainty tugging at him. He excused himself to pass most crust-less sandwiches and tea. He kept one hand free for the violin under his arm. "Dad, will this be over soon?"

"I would think so," Joe smiled. "Everyone's had seconds. They'll go soon."

The phone rang. Devon handed Joe the violin and went to answer it. The caller wanted Mel who returned a few minutes later with a puzzled smile on her face. She pulled Joe to one side, out of hearing distance from the guests.

"That was the police. They've arrested Dono." Her eyes opened wide. "They said they got a search warrant because my father gave them information that was enough to secure the warrant. They said Dono resisted arrest, punched an officer, so they've got him on that too."

"Wow," Joe said. "That's great. That's a relief."

"They searched his office and his apartment. They found methamphetamines in the apartment as well as all kinds of his work records. They said Allison is going to testify." Mel fingered the corner of her eyes. "I'm *so* relieved. It means I don't have to hide anymore. I don't have to worry about Ty. Oh, Joe, you don't know what this means to me."

"I think I know," he smiled. "Owen said he'd look after his family."

"What …?" Incredulous.

"Your father told me to look after *my* family and he'd take care of *his*. I guess that's what he's done."

Mel was thoughtful, shaking her head. "He did it for us?"

"Why else would he do it? He's got nothing else to gain."

Mel's eyes teared and she gulped back a sob. "Oh, Joe," she said. Joe drew her against his chest and Mel sobbed for a minute, overwhelmed by feelings.

"Wait 'till I tell Mum," Mel said, wiping her eyes. "She'll feel vindicated."

Joe gave her a fierce hug and a light kiss. "This is great, Mel."

Mel went to find her mother in the kitchen. Scott came over to Joe and said he and Marion were going to leave soon. Joe took him aside and told him about Dono. Scott smiled his pleasure. "That miserable S.O.B. finally got his!"

"Uh, before you go, Scott, can I see you tomorrow to talk business?"

"Sure. You're getting closer to selling the house? It's looking pretty good, by the way."

"Yeah, I want to talk to you about that and about buying something," Joe said.

"Buying something?"

"Yeah. Maybe you can convince me I should buy the house on Little Bear Lake." Joe smiled.

Scott stood back and looked at Joe squarely. "That's the best idea I've heard all summer," he beamed. He looked towards Mel who was talking to her mother. "Great idea," he repeated.

The phone rang again. Devon answered it and stayed on the line a long time. "Mom," he said when he got back. "Just wanted to see if we're okay."

Joe raised his eyebrows. "Nice," he said.

"She thinks it's time I came home," Devon said.

"What do you think?"

Devon shrugged. "You don't have much longer here, do you?"

"About a week, give or take," Joe said.

"Then I go this week, I guess."

"I guess it's nearly over." They looked at each other, sifted through their thoughts for a minute.

"Do you think Gram can get slushies, wherever she is?"

Joe nodded. "I'll bet there's music, too."

Three days later Joe and Devon stood at the security gate at the Vancouver airport. The violin case was tucked under Devon's arm. The skateboard had been checked into special baggage. Joe asked Devon, once again, if he had his boarding pass and ID. Joe was telling him he'd see him in Toronto in less than a week.

"Do you think we could have another summer like this sometime?" Devon asked. "Because, even with Gram and everything …."

"The first time only happens once, Dev. But if it's special enough it lasts forever." Devon's flight was called and he was gone.

As Joe drove the hour from Vancouver International Airport to Chilliwack, he mused about the possibility of bidding on Vancouver as his home base. Devon wouldn't even mind him not being in Toronto if it meant they had the Little Bear Lake house. He'd talked to Scott and it could happen. Soon he was pulling into Nathan's care facility parking lot. Now, he knew how to buzz himself in. Catherine waved at him from her office. He keyed the code for the door to Nathan's unit. Several people with vacant faces wandered the hallway. One stopped at the desk and asked the nurse if the bus had come yet. Joe continued along the corridor to room 12.

Nathan was sitting in his chair, tearing pages from a magazine. When Joe stopped at the door, Nathan looked up. "Will?" he said.

"Dad, I'm Joe. Your son, Joe."

Nathan looked confused, agitated, his hands fluttered over the pages of the magazine. Torn pages littered the floor.

Joe entered the room and looked at Nathan in silence. Then said, "Did you know she forgave us, Dad? She forgave each of us."

"Will? Is that you?"

Joe turned to the window, hands in pocket and inhaled deeply. He turned around, withdrew a package from his pocket and extended it to Nathan.

"Yes, it's Will. Look — I've brought gummie bears."

ISBN 142515585-5